MYTH·O·MANIA

IX

UNDERWORLD LIBRARY
ANCIENT GREECE

AUTHOR
Kate McMullan

TITLE
Hit the Road, Helen!

DATE DUE	BORROWER'S NAME	
XXVII	*Lord Hades*	
XXXI	*Lord Hades*	

Myth-O-Mania is published by Stone Arch Books
A Capstone Imprint
1710 Roe Crest Drive
North Mankato, Minnesota 56003
www.capstoneyoungreaders.com

Text copyright © 2013 by Kate McMullan

*Library of Congress Cataloging-in-Publication Data is available on the
Library of Congress website.*

Library binding: 978-1-4342-4990-6 · Paper Over Board: 978-1-4342-6219-6

Summary: Hades sets the record straight on the true story of the Trojan War.

Cover Illustration: Kevin Keele
Cover, Map, and Interior Design: Kristi Carlson
Production Specialist: Eric Manske

Image Credits:
Shutterstock: B. McQueen, Cre8tive Images, Natalia Barsukova, NY–P,
osov, Pablo H. Caridad, Perov Stanislav, Petrov Stanislav Eduardovich,
Selena. Author photo: Phill Lehans

Printed in China by Nordica.
0413/CA21300515
032013   007226NORDF13

MYTH-O-MANIA
IX

HIT THE ROAD,
HELEN!

BY
KATE McMULLAN

STONE ARCH BOOKS
a capstone imprint

N

THESSALY

GREECE

AEGEAN
SEA

Troy

Delphi
Thebes
Athens

ITHACA

PELOPONNESE

Olympia

Sparta

CRETE

ANCIENT
Greece!

UNDERWORLD · MAP · CORPORATION

 Mount Olympus   Aulis Harbor

 Menelaus's Palace   Odysseus's Home

Priam's Palace   Hades's Underworld Entrance

TABLE OF CONTENTS

PROLOGUE 7

CHAPTER I: Two Blue Eggs 15

CHAPTER II: Three Weddings 29

CHAPTER III: For The Fairest........................... 42

CHAPTER IV: A Dip In The Styx 58

CHAPTER V: Go Back! Go Back!......................73

CHAPTER VI: The Oath 91

CHAPTER VII: A Thousand Ships...................... 105

CHAPTER VIII: Taking Sides................................ 120

CHAPTER IX: War!...133

CHAPTER X: Ghost Stories 148

CHAPTER XI: Achilles's Armor 159

CHAPTER XII: Meanwhile, In The Underworld............171

CHAPTER XIII: The Bow Of Hercules 182

CHAPTER XIV: The Trojan Horse 197

EPILOGUE 214

KING HADES'S QUICK-AND-EASY
GUIDE TO THE MYTHS...224

PROLOGUE

Greetings, mortals! It's me, Hades, Ruler of the Underworld, here to give you the lowdown on the lady known as Helen of Troy.

You think you know her story? Think again.

The reason I'm so sure you *don't* is a four-letter word that starts with Z and ends with S.

Wild guess?

You got it.

Zeus.

How'd you like it if *your* little brother were Ruler of the Universe? Welcome to my world. Zeus *is* my little brother. Wait. Make that my *younger* brother, because *little* isn't really accurate. Not with that potbelly he's got going. And his backside? One look and you'll know why he has to order his togas doublewide.

Zeus became Ruler of the Universe by cheating at cards. Once he had the top spot, he started trying to control everything. The weather. The seasons. How many loops in a pretzel. He even started messing with the myths.

Zeus had his nymphs comb through *The Big Fat Book of Greek Myths*, take out all the ridiculous things he did, and replace them with stories that made him seem strong and powerful. So there's Zeus on practically every page, hurling lightning bolts at two-headed giants. Or thundering away at sea monsters.

Lies, lies, lies!

Take it from me: when real trouble comes along, brave-and-mighty Zeus has been known to morph into a pigeon and fly away.

Don't believe me? Just take a look at what he had those re-write nymphs write about Helen of Troy:

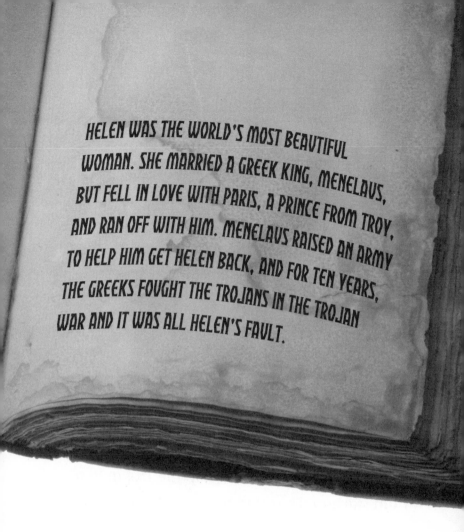

HELEN WAS THE WORLD'S MOST BEAUTIFUL WOMAN. SHE MARRIED A GREEK KING, MENELAUS, BUT FELL IN LOVE WITH PARIS, A PRINCE FROM TROY, AND RAN OFF WITH HIM. MENELAUS RAISED AN ARMY TO HELP HIM GET HELEN BACK, AND FOR TEN YEARS, THE GREEKS FOUGHT THE TROJANS IN THE TROJAN WAR AND IT WAS ALL HELEN'S FAULT.

Zeus left out one little detail. It's a five-letter word that begins with A and ends with W.

Did you say *arrow*?

Nice one.

Because of a cowardly act by Zeus — which I'll tell you ALL about right here in this book — Cupid shot Helen with a love arrow just as Paris showed up. *ZING!*

If Cupid hadn't shot that arrow, Helen would never have run off with Paris. And the Trojan War would never have happened.

War is a terrible thing for mortals. Many of them lose their lives. And for what? Often something that could be settled with just a good talk.

War is a terrible thing for me, too. My Underworld kingdom fills up with way too many ghosts. There isn't room for them all, and it's a mess.

I tried my godly best to stop the Trojan War from starting. The effort took years and years off of my life, and in the end, I still couldn't manage to stop it.

That's partly because I don't believe in interfering too much in the lives of mortals. They get in enough trouble on their own without us gods and goddesses sticking our noses in and making things worse. But lots of other immortals don't feel this way — at all!

So Zeus, Aphrodite, Apollo, and other assorted immortals helped the Trojans, while Hera, Athena, Poseidon, and others helped the Greeks. And with the gods taking sides like that, the war went on and on and on.

Zeus dumped all the blame for the war on Helen. He did it because he was afraid that if mortals found out it was *his* fault, they might stop sending him smoky sacrifices. They might stop worshipping at his temples. They might wake up and realize that Zeus is nothing but a myth-o-maniac, old Greek speak for "big fat liar."

You want the real scoop on Helen and the Trojan War? It's a great story. But put your feet up and make yourself comfortable, because it's long and complicated, filled with spiteful gods and goddesses, quarreling warriors, and lots of seers predicting the future.

Just look at the major players:

Major Players in the Trojan War

The Greeks:

- **AGAMEMNON** — high king of Greece
- **MENELAUS** — Agamemnon's brother, king of Sparta
- **HELEN** — wife of Menelaus
- **ACHILLES** — greatest hero
- **ODYSSEUS** — cleverest hero
- **NESTOR** — wise old hero
- **CALCHAS** — soothsayer

Immortals for the Greeks:

- **ATHENA** — goddess of war and wisdom
- **HEPHAESTUS** — god of the forge
- **HERA** — queen of the gods
- **POSEIDON** — god of the sea
- **THETIS** — sea goddess; mother of Achilles

THE TROJANS:

- **PRIAM** — king of Troy
- **HECTOR** — Priam's son, great hero
- **PARIS** — Priam's good-looking son
- **CASSANDRA** — Priam's prophesying daughter
- **SARPEDON** — mortal son of Zeus

IMMORTALS FOR THE TROJANS:

- **APHRODITE** — goddess of love and beauty
- **APOLLO** — sun god
- **ZEUS** — myth-o-maniac and king of the gods

Poor Helen. She was basically a prisoner behind the walls of Troy during the war, so she missed out on lots of the action. But Helen's name is stamped on the story — Helen of Troy, the face that launched a thousand ships — so that's how I'll tell it.

I have to start way back before Helen was born. I'll bet you know how it all begins, don't you?

Sure you do.

With that Z-word.

CHAPTER 1

TWO BLUE EGGS

Zeus had a bad habit of falling in love with mortal women, so it wasn't a big surprise when he fell for Leda. She was a beauty, known all over Greece for her lovely white arms. Not a great accomplishment in my book, but you work with what you've got, and what Leda had was white arms.

I happened to be with Zeus when he first spotted Leda. I'd driven my bride, Persephone, up to earth so she could carry out her goddess-of-spring duties. You know, making flowers bloom and trees sprout leaves. That's what she does for half of the year. The other half she spends with me as Queen of the Underworld.

I'd just dropped her off at a friend's house in the Greek city of Sparta when I caught sight of Zeus standing by the side of the road. I tried to make a quick U-turn before he spotted me, but I was too late.

"Hey, Hades!" he yelled, waving and flagging me down.

Busted! I drove my chariot over to him and stopped.

"Good thing you came by," Zeus said climbing into the passenger seat, which I had not invited him to do. "My chariot broke an axel. Now you can give me a lift over to the Sparta Spa."

"Giddy-up, Harley! Giddy-up, Davidson!" I called to my steeds. The sooner I got him there, the sooner I'd be rid of him.

"You should see the massage nymphs at this spa, Hades," Zeus went on. "Real lookers. And they do this whole scalp massage thing. Guaranteed to grow hair."

I glanced over at Zeus's balding dome. It was going to take a lot more than a massage to stop his hair loss.

"Whoa!" Zeus shouted suddenly, and my team slowed down.

"I thought you wanted to go to the spa," I said.

Zeus didn't answer. His bulging eyes were riveted on a beautiful woman walking along the road with some of her serving maids.

I took a closer look and recognized Leda. She was a friend of Persephone's, and over the years, I'd gotten to know her, too.

"Look at those white arms!" exclaimed Zeus. "Who is she? I'm going to marry her!"

"That's Leda," I said. "And you're already married to Hera, Zeus."

"Leda's gorgeous," Zeus grunted.

"Leda's married, too," I added. "King Tyndareus of Sparta is her husband."

"You think I give a fig?" said Zeus. "Let me out of this chariot!"

"Aw, Zeus," I said. "Leda and Tyndareus are

happy together. Persephone tells me they're about to start a family. Leave her alone."

"STOP THIS CHARIOT!" Zeus bellowed.

I reined in Harley and Davidson.

Zeus hopped out, calling, "Mortal woman! White-armed mortal woman!" and I knew he'd already forgotten her name.

I watched my little brother bound toward Leda, thinking that if he got any broader in the backside, he wasn't even going to fit into a doublewide.

I didn't run into Zeus for a while after that. But word on the street had it that he was hanging around the palace in Sparta, flirting shamelessly with Leda.

Word also had it that Leda wasn't interested. She was happy being married to Tyndareus and happy being Queen of Sparta. Besides, having white arms didn't make her stupid. She knew that Zeus would bring her nothing but trouble.

* * *

When Persephone's away, I spend my evenings at Villa Pluto, my Underworld palace, hanging out with my three-headed pooch, Cerberus, and watching wrestling on TV.

One night, I sat down in my La-Z-God recliner in the den, ready to watch the big match between my favorite competitor, 'Eagle-Eye' Cyclops, and Python, the Giant Snake. That Python was a wily one, always ready with the squeeze play. I hoped Cyclops could keep an eye on him.

I had a VI-pack of Necta-Colas chilling in a cooler and a piping hot ambrosia-and-pepperoni pie from Underworld Pizza. I picked up the remote and clicked on the TV.

A giant image of Zeus's face appeared on my screen. I clicked like crazy, trying to get to the Wrestling Channel, but I was stuck on the Zeus Channel — all Zeus, all the time.

I stared at the screen. What was the king of the gods up to now? Zeus seemed to be huddled in the clouds on Mount Olympus, peering down at the earth.

The scene shifted to show what Zeus was

looking at. He was spying on Leda! There she was, all alone on the shore of a lake, feeding the swans.

Once more Zeus's face filled the screen, and I could tell the old master of the quick disguise was having a brainstorm. He vanished from the clouds. The scene shifted again, and I saw that a really big swan had joined the flock on the shore of Leda's lake.

If only Leda had looked closely at that swan! She might have noticed that it had a potbelly. And was missing lots of feathers on the top of its head.

But Leda just smiled and tossed the new swan some extra pita crumbs. The swan strutted around like the big feather-covered show-off that it was.

Leda laughed and said, "I've never seen such a fine swan!"

Ichor is the golden fluid that we immortals have coursing through our veins instead of blood, and watching Zeus the swan made my ichor boil! I clicked the remote again. It worked, giving me a close-up of Eagle-Eye Cyclops about to pin Python to the mat. This was more like it!

"Go, Cyclops!" I cheered, reaching for a Necta-Cola and forcing all thoughts of Zeus from my mind. "Pin that snake!"

* * *

It's not so easy being King of the Underworld. There's so much to do. I try to be on the banks of the River Styx when Hermes arrives driving his rattletrap bus filled with new ghosts. I supervise Charon, the River Taxi driver, who ferries the ghosts across the Styx to my Underworld kingdom. And it's up to me to make sure that my staff keeps Motel Styx, the temporary quarters for new arrivals, clean and ready for ghosts to stay there until they're judged.

After the judging, I see to it that the ghosts of the good are sent to the peaceful apple orchards of blue-skied Elysium. I point the ghosts of the not so good toward the drab, gray Asphodel Fields, where they wander for eternity. It's also my duty to send the ghosts of the wicked to Tartarus, where eternal flames burn and smoky volcanoes spew red-hot lava.

Persephone understands how hard I work. In the evenings, when she's around, she'll bring out a deck of cards or a board game, something calming to take my mind off my kingly duties.

And yet one night when my queen and I were sitting together in the den, having a game of Scrabble, Persephone told me something extremely un-relaxing.

"Hades," she said, "we've been invited to a dinner party."

"We're busy, P-phone." I put down tiles to spell the word *NO*.

"You don't even know when it is." Persephone played the word *ACCEPT*.

"Doesn't matter," I said, studying the board.

"It's next week," said Persephone. "Leda and Tyndareus have invited us to their palace. I want to go, Hades. Please? I think Leda has big news."

I groaned. In those days, it wasn't unusual for gods and mortals to be good friends. But eating mortal food is such a drag. We gods have to sprinkle on tons of Ambro-salts to make it taste like anything and get the Ambrosia we need to keep us looking young and godly.

I used the *A* from *ACCEPT* to spell out *BLAH.*

"That's not a word, Hades," said Persephone. "But I'll let it count if we can go."

I watched her put down the rest of her tiles to spell *GODDESS.*

"I win, Hades!" she cheered.

I sighed. "You always do."

* * *

The next week, Persephone and I traveled up to the royal palace in Sparta. Servants took our godly coats and led us to the dining hall.

"Welcome, welcome!" King Tyndareus greeted us happily.

"So good of you to come!" Leda added.

One look at her, and we knew her big news.

"Leda!" exclaimed Persephone. "You're going to have a baby!"

Leda smiled. "I wanted to tell you in person," she said.

"That's wonderful!" cried Persephone. "Isn't it, Hades?" She elbowed me in the side.

"Uh, yes!" I managed. "Great news!"

Tyndareus was beaming. "Our first child!" he exclaimed.

Just then Leda put a hand to her stomach. "Oh, my!" she said.

"Leda!" said Tyndareus. "Is it time?"

"I'm not sure," said Leda. "Maybe I'll go lie down in the Birthing Room for a moment."

Persephone took her arm. "I'll come with you," she said.

Tyndareus and I were deep into a discussion about the upcoming Wrestle Dome match between Eagle-Eye and Stinger the Scorpion when Persephone raced back, shouting, "Somebody get the midwife!"

"Hurry!" Leda called from the Birthing Room. "Whoops!" she added. "Never mind."

"You mean you had the baby?" called Tyndareus.

"You'd better come in here," Leda called back to her husband.

Tyndareus ran to the Birthing Room. Persephone and I were right behind him. We all skidded to a halt in the doorway.

There was Leda, sitting on the bed, looking confused. Beside her were two big blue eggs.

"Uh . . ." said Tyndareus. Now *he* looked confused. "Where's our baby?"

"Inside the eggs?" said Leda.

"Ah!" Tyndareus nodded, as if this sort of thing happened every day.

"I'd better keep them warm," said Leda, pulling the eggs closer and sitting on them as best she could. "I wonder when they'll hatch."

"You two need some time alone," I said, grabbing Persephone's elbow and pulling her from the room. "We'll keep in touch!"

Persephone and I hopped into my chariot and headed back to the Underworld, where we had a tasty dinner at the de Minos Grill.

While we ate, we talked about Leda and those big blue eggs. Persephone didn't know what to make of them, but I had a bad feeling about those eggs. A very bad feeling.

* * *

Persephone and I went up to Sparta each week to check on Leda. Every visit, we found her sitting on those eggs, but they showed no signs of hatching.

Summer's a busy time for Persephone. She has to make sure the apple blossoms are turning into apples and the plum blossoms are turning into plums. So one night I went to see Tyndareus and Leda on my own. As soon as I arrived at the palace, I could tell that something was up. A servant ushered me into what was now called the Hatching Room.

"Welcome, Hades!" said Tyndareus.

Leda got up from her little nest to greet me and suddenly, *CRRRRRAAACK!* One of the eggs split open, and two little babies tumbled out.

"So sweet," cooed Leda, picking them up. "They look just like you, Tyndareus."

"So they do!" Tyndareus smiled. "Let's call the boy Castor and the girl Clytemnestra."

"Beautiful names," murmured Leda.

"Nice work," I muttered, not knowing what to say.

Now the other egg began rolling around. It made a real racket. *CRRRRRAAAAACK!* Two more babies tumbled out of that egg, another boy and another girl.

"They don't look like me, do they?" Tyndareus said.

"Not much," agreed Leda.

I took one look at the boy baby and thought, *Uh-oh.*

Tyndareus and Leda named that pair Pollux and Helen.

"Helen's a pretty little thing," said Tyndareus. "But Pollux is a bit beefy. And look! He's got a potbelly." He stared at Pollux and at last he said, "Do you think Zeus could be his father?"

"Anything's possible," said Leda. "But if Pollux and Helen are Zeus's children, let's not tell them, Tyndareus."

"Never," Tyndareus agreed. "We'll treat all four babies alike. Perhaps in time, we shall forget about Zeus."

Good luck with that, I thought tiptoeing out of the Hatching Room.

But Tyndareus and Leda were true to their word. Helen and Clytemnestra were best friends and so were Castor and Pollux. All four children grew up in Tyndareus's court together, never knowing about those big blue eggs.

CHAPTER II

THREE WEDDINGS

In the coming years, whenever I traveled up to earth, I'd stop by Sparta to talk wrestling with King Tyndareus. I spent time with Leda, too, and got to know the kids.

Clytemnestra and Castor were fine-looking children. Pollux looked just like Zeus, but Helen lucked out and didn't look a thing like him. With her golden hair, blue eyes, and cheeks as pink as the dawn, she was a stunner. When Helen walked down the street, heads turned — sometimes so quickly that half the population of Sparta ended up with stiff necks.

Helen didn't seem to give a fig whether people found her beautiful or not. All she cared about was sitting in her Loom Room spinning wool into yarn and weaving that yarn into tapestries.

"Clytemnestra's our social butterfly, and Helen's our artist," her mother told everyone proudly.

When Clytemnestra let it be known that she wished to marry, her parents chose Agamemnon, High King of Greece, to be her husband.

Agamemnon had a thick black beard. He was big and loud and was always starting fights. I didn't like him much, but Clytemnestra seemed crazy about him.

Tyndareus and Leda invited Persephone and me to the wedding, and we pretty much had to go. Persephone made herself a gown out of buttercups for the occasion.

"You look like a million bucks, P-phone," I told her.

"Thanks, Hades!" she said. "Here's a little surprise for you."

She handed me a new toga tux. I didn't really

want to wear the thing. I'm not big on being buttoned up. But I put it on and checked myself in the mirror. Not bad!

When we arrived at the palace for the wedding, I slipped the usher a fiver to seat us in the back. Persephone didn't mind sitting at the back because it meant she'd be among the first to see Helen, the world's most beautiful bridesmaid, walking down the aisle, followed by the lovely bride, Clytemnestra.

Sitting in the rear also made it easy for me to slip away to Tyndareus's den and check on the match at Wrestle Dome. That night, Eagle-Eye was going up against Hydra, a foul-smelling, nine-headed swamp monster. Hydra had eighteen eyes to Eagle-Eye's one. It didn't seem like a fair match.

After the ceremony, we went to the reception and Persephone insisted that we dance. Across the floor, I spied Helen dancing with Agamemnon's red-haired younger brother, Menelaus. She was smiling at him, and he smiled back in a shy sort of way as if he couldn't believe that someone as gorgeous as Helen was giving him the time of day.

Menelaus didn't seem much like his brash older brother. He and Helen looked happy together, and I wondered if Leda and Tyndareus would soon be throwing another wedding.

When the band took a break, Persephone beckoned Helen over.

"You were a beautiful bridesmaid!" Persephone exclaimed. "You and Menelaus seem to be having a good time together," she added. "What do you like about him?"

"His red hair," Helen said. "I'm going to dye my next batch of yarn exactly that color."

When the two of us were on our way home, Persephone said, "Helen likes the color of his hair? I guess it's a start."

"What do you like about me, P-phone?" I asked her.

"Everything, Hades." She flashed me a smile. "Absolutely everything."

* * *

Word of Helen's beauty spread far and wide. Many suitors traveled to Sparta to woo her. Many, *many* suitors. I saw them for myself one day when I was visiting the palace.

"Come have a look at Helen's suitors, Hades," Leda said, leading me over to a window in the dining hall.

I saw hundreds of young men camped out on the palace grounds.

"Kings from every little island in the Aegean Sea have come to court Helen," added Tyndareus.

"If we pick one to be Helen's husband, the others will be angry," said Leda. "They might start fighting."

"I wish they'd all go home," said Tyndareus. "Helen doesn't even seem to care about getting married."

I looked out again at the sea of suitors. I spotted red-haired Menelaus in the crowd. I also saw Philoctetes, the famous archer to whom Hercules had given his bow and his poison-tipped arrows. At the edge of the crowd, I spied the king of Ithaca, Odysseus, he of the short legs and broad shoulders. The two of us went way back.

"Odysseus is clever," I told Tyndareus. "He might be able to help you out."

Tyndareus and I strode out to the palace yard to talk to Odysseus. Right away the suitors started showing off in hopes of impressing Helen's dad. Some did push-ups. Others sang songs. Still others demonstrated their sword-fighting skills.

"It's a nightmare," Tyndareus muttered.

We found Odysseus sitting on a rock.

"Lord Hades!" he exclaimed, hopping up when he saw me.

"Odysseus, my man," I said. "How come you're not showing off for King Tyndareus here?"

"The truth is, I'm not so sure I want to marry Helen," Odysseus replied.

"Why not?" cried Tyndareus.

"Don't get me wrong," Odysseus said. "Helen's a real babe. But being married to her would be a never-ending battle to fend off other guys." He shook his head. "I don't want to spend my life fighting off the competition."

"You're a wise man, Odysseus," said Tyndareus. "Can you help us come up with a plan for choosing Helen's husband and dealing with the disappointed suitors?"

Odysseus jumped back up onto the rock and looked around, sizing up the situation. He thought for a while and jumped down.

"Here's what you do, Tyndareus," he said, and keeping his voice low, he told us his plan.

"Very clever," Tyndareus said. "It just might work."

I phoned Persephone and told her not to expect me home for dinner. No way was I taking off before Tyndareus carried out the plan.

Thinking that I might be a distraction for the suitors, seeing as how I was a god and all, I decided to do my disappearing act. I took out my magical wallet, a gift from Persephone. She'd had it monogrammed with my initials, K.H.R.O.T.U. — King Hades, Ruler of the Underworld. The amazing thing about the wallet is that it stretches to hold whatever I put inside, then shrinks back down to wallet-size again so

I can slip it into my pocket. When it comes to giving gifts, Persephone's a genius.

I opened the wallet and took out my Helmet of Darkness. That had been a gift, too, from my Cyclopes uncles. When I put the Helmet on — POOF! — I vanish. And so does whatever I'm holding.

King Tyndareus hurried back into the palace. Before long, he, Leda, and a servant appeared on a balcony. Unseen, I stepped out behind them as the servant banged on a gong.

"Attention, suitors!" King Tyndareus shouted to the crowd.

The suitors all quieted immediately.

"Queen Leda and I are about to choose one of you to be Helen's husband," Tyndareus said. "If you wish to be considered, you must promise to accept our choice without argument."

The suitors grumbled among themselves. At last King Menelaus shouted, "I accept!" The archer Philoctetes called, "I accept!" Finally all the other kings shouted it, too: "I accept! I accept!"

"You must also swear a sacred oath to obey the man we choose as Helen's husband," Tyndareus continued, "no matter what he asks."

Hearing this, the suitors grumbled even louder than before.

Philoctetes the archer shouted, "What sort of thing might he ask?"

Tyndareus was ready with his answer. "If any man should steal Helen away, he might ask you to join forces and fight to win her back," he said. "And you must do so!"

There was more grumbling from the suitors, but no one left. Every man wanted to stay, hoping he would be the chosen one.

At last red-haired Menelaus shouted, "I swear to the oath!"

And all the suitors quickly shouted, "I swear! I swear!"

"You have all sworn to uphold the oath," Tyndareus said. "Leda? The envelope please."

Leda handed him an envelope. Tyndareus ripped it open and pulled out a slip of parchment. "The husband is . . ."

The servant banged out a gong roll.

"King Menelaus of Mycenae!" shouted Tyndareus.

There was no clapping or cheering. The losing suitors only muttered, "Aw, man!" and milled around, slapping each other on the back in sympathy.

"When's the wedding?" called out one of the losing suitors.

"We all get to come, right?" called another.

"Invite them, Tyndareus," Leda whispered to her husband. "Otherwise they might start fighting."

Tyndareus thought quickly. "Uh . . . the wedding is . . . uh . . . tomorrow!" he shouted. "You're all invited!"

At that, the crowd clapped and whooped. There's nothing like the promise of a big party to cheer up an unhappy suitor.

* * *

The wedding went off without a hitch.

Helen wore Clytemnestra's wedding gown, and Menelaus wore his suitor suit.

"They look happy, don't they, Hades?" asked Persephone. She'd traveled up to Sparta for the wedding and looked smashing in her buttercup gown.

"Very happy," I agreed.

At the reception, servants kept topping off the suitors' wine cups, and everyone was having a fine time. But Tyndareus had the best time of all. Both of his daughters were married, and after the reception, all the suitors would be gone.

As I stood talking to Odysseus, Tyndareus came over.

"Clever plan, Odysseus," he said. "Very clever. How can I ever thank you?"

Odysseus nodded toward a dark-haired young woman in the crowd. "Introduce me to her," he said.

"Gladly." Tyndareus motioned the young woman over. "This is Penelope, Helen's cousin," he said. "Penelope, meet King Odysseus of Ithaca."

"Hi ya, King," said Penelope with a sly smile.

Odysseus broke into a grin, and I knew what he was thinking. Penelope was lovely, but not lovely enough to cause problems with other suitors.

"Wanna dance?" Odysseus asked.

"Totally," said Penelope.

Before the evening was out, Odysseus had asked Penelope to marry him. (I was standing two feet away at the bar and couldn't help but overhear.)

"Do you like to travel?" Penelope asked him.

"Not that much," said Odysseus.

"Good," said Penelope. "I'd really hate to have a husband who was away for long stretches of time."

"Nah," said Odysseus. "I'm a regular homebody."

Tyndareus slipped the priest a few more drachmas, and he agreed to marry Odysseus and Penelope in front of all the guests still standing. The next day, the couple sailed off for Ithaca together.

"It seems like yesterday that Helen hatched out of that big blue egg," Persephone said as we headed home to the Underworld. "And now she's married."

"Time flies," I said, hoping we wouldn't be invited to another wedding for a few hundred years.

CHAPTER III

FOR THE FAIREST

No wedding invitations arrived at Villa Pluto for years and years.

During those years, Leda and Tyndareus stepped down from their thrones, and Helen and Menelaus became the new queen and king of Sparta. In time, they had a daughter of their own, Hermione. They were happy in Sparta. And every day, Helen wove tapestries with yarn as blue as the sea, as gold as the sun, and as red as Menelaus's hair.

I know this because I visited Tyndareus from

time to time, and I saw the palace walls become increasingly draped with Helen's work. Every chair and stool was topped with a woven pillow. Every table was covered with a woven cloth.

Helen was as beautiful as ever. But her tapestries? Not so much. All those bright reds and blues and golds were hard on the eyes.

One day when I'd stopped by the palace to see Tyndareus, Helen caught up with me in a hallway. "Hades!" she said. "Have you seen my latest work?" She gestured at the tapestry-covered walls. "I'd love to weave something for you and Persephone."

"Uh . . ." What could I say? Persephone is really picky about what we hang on the walls at Villa Pluto.

"I could show a volcano spewing bright red lava," Helen went on, warming to the idea.

"Let me get back to you on that," I said, hurrying away to the Underworld without saying yes.

* * *

Centuries ago, when I was just a teen god, I promised my mom, Rhea, that I'd look after my youngest brother, Zeus, and I spend a huge chunk of my time straightening out his messes. But for a long stretch, everything on earth was peaceful. It was so peaceful for so long that I began to wonder — what was Zeus up to? He didn't seem to be causing trouble.

I didn't know it at the time, but Zeus was about to make his biggest mess *ever*. My peaceful time was about to come to a screeching halt. And so was Helen's.

* * *

One evening after work, I was chilling in my La-Z-God, watching my favorite bio-pic, *Eagle-Eye: One-Eyed Wonder*. Persephone was sitting nearby, sorting through the mail.

"Look, Hades," she said, holding up a big fancy envelope. "Wedding time!"

I groaned softly as she opened it.

"Listen to this!" she said.

> **"IMMORTAL ZEUS,**
> **THUNDER GOD,**
> **HURLER OF LIGHTNING BOLTS,**
> **RULER OF THE UNIVERSE . . ."**

"That's a wedding invitation?" I said. "It sounds more like Zeus's résumé."

"Just listen," said Persephone.

> **"ZEUS,** *yadda, yadda, yadda,*
> **INVITES YOU TO THE MARRIAGE CEREMONY OF**
> **PELEUS, KING OF THESSALY**
> **AND**
> **THETIS, IMMORTAL SEA GODDESS."**

"Thetis is getting married?" I asked.

"Apparently." Persephone scanned the invitation. "There's more about a big blow-out party following the wedding." She looked up at me. "Thetis is a powerful Nereid," she said. "Why is she marrying some lowly mortal king?"

"Peleus isn't just any mortal king. He's the commander of the famous Myrmidon army,"

I told her. "The real question is why Zeus is throwing the wedding."

"I'm calling Aphrodite." Persephone picked up her phone and headed for the porch. "The goddess of love will know what's going on."

"Take your time, P-phone," I called after her. I gave Cerbie's heads a triple rub and started *One-Eyed Wonder*. It was just ending when Persephone returned. She sat down across from me on the couch.

"Aphrodite says that Zeus saw silver-footed Thetis running over the ocean waves and fell madly in love with her," Persephone said.

"Silver-footed Thetis?" I said. "That's worse than white-armed Leda."

"Well, Thetis can race over the sea faster than any other sea goddess," Persephone said. "Anyway, Zeus chased after Thetis for months. He finally asked her to marry him, and Thetis said yes."

My little brother had gotten married more times than I could count.

"Zeus was so happy that he ran around

telling everyone that he and Thetis were getting married," Persephone went on. "And Thetis's father, Nereus, found out. You know him, Hades."

I nodded. "The Old Man of the Sea."

"Right," said Persephone. "Nereus appeared to Zeus and said, 'What about the prophecy?' And Zeus said, 'What prophecy?' And Nereus said, 'Thetis shall bear a son who is mightier than his father.' And Zeus said, 'Whoa! No wonder she's still single!'"

"So Zeus called off the wedding?" I guessed.

"You got it, Hades," said Persephone. "But Zeus didn't want Thetis telling everyone that he'd jilted her, so when he heard that Peleus was looking for a wife, he fixed him up with Thetis. Peleus is thrilled."

"What about Thetis?" I asked.

"She didn't want to marry a mortal," Persephone said, "but then — *ZING!*"

"*ZING?*" I cried. "You mean —"

"Yep," said Persephone. "Zeus had Cupid shoot her with a love arrow."

"So Thetis fell in love with Peleus," I said. "And Zeus is so happy to be off the hook that he's throwing the wedding."

"Exactly," said Persephone. "Aphrodite says the wedding's going to be huge. Zeus has invited lots of mortals and all of us gods and goddesses, too. Well, all of us except for Eris."

"What?" I cranked my La-Z-God straight upright. "Eris is the only immortal not invited?"

"That's right," said Persephone. "She *is* the goddess of discord, Hades. Who wants everybody fighting at a wedding?"

"Zeus can't leave her out!" I stood up and started pacing back and forth in the den. "Eris is going to find out about the wedding. And she'll know she's the only one he didn't invite."

"So?" said Persephone. "When you're a goddess who makes trouble, you have to expect not to be invited to parties."

"This is going to cause problems, Persephone," I said. "Big problems!"

"Oh, lighten up, Hades," said Persephone. "This calls for a new gown!"

Hey, mortal readers. You don't think I've forgotten that the title of this book is *Hit the Road, Helen!*, do you? Not a chance. Stick with me here. You'll see. The wedding, the uninvited Eris. It all leads back to Helen.

* * *

For this wedding, Persephone made herself a gown out of violets. It was beautiful, and it smelled good, too. I'd put on a few pounds since Helen's wedding, but I managed to squeeze into my toga tux.

When the day of the wedding rolled around, Persephone and I drove up to earth. We took our places at the ceremony with the other immortals.

Peleus appeared, and Thetis started down the aisle.

"Peleus is handsome, Hades!" Persephone whispered. "And doesn't Thetis look gorgeous in that sea-foam gown?"

"Hmm," I answered, looking around nervously. I half expected Eris to burst in and make a scene, but all went well.

After the wedding, we filed into a huge tent for the reception.

"Eat! Drink! Party!" Zeus barked as we entered, holding a big stinky cigar between his teeth. I tried to dodge him, but he caught up with me by the lobster-roll platters.

"This is the wedding of the century, huh, Hades?" Zeus said, elbowing me in the side. "Cost me a fortune. Check the sea nymphs working the buffet." He waggled his cigar. "Ever see such cute little guppies?"

Persephone swept between us and grabbed my elbow. "Let's try the shrimp!" she said.

"Thanks, P-phone," I murmured as we made our getaway. We stood by the shrimp tower, looking out at all the major gods and goddesses. There were minor deities, too — muses, water sprites, moon goddesses — as well as a smattering of mortal kings and queens.

"Hera looks great in red," said Persephone.

"And that golden gown really suits Aphrodite, don't you think?"

"Oh, yeah," I replied, helping myself to more shrimp.

"That blue dress looks lovely on Athena." Persephone sighed. "But just for one night, couldn't she leave the helmet at home?"

"Here come Tyndareus and Leda," I said, pointing across the room.

"And Menelaus and —" Persephone stopped and stared. "What is Helen wearing?"

I saw that Helen had on a blue, gold, and red dress that fit her like, well, like a wall hanging.

"She must have woven it herself, poor dear," said Persephone. "Even so, she looks gorgeous. I'm going to talk to her."

As she hurried off, someone called, "Hades!"

I turned to see Odysseus and Penelope coming toward me.

"What a shindig, huh?" said Odysseus.

"We haven't been to a good party in ages," Penelope added. "Not since our son, Telemachus, was born."

As we chatted, I started to relax. What a worrywart I'd been about Eris. And all for nothing! But just as I let my guard down, a commotion broke out at the entrance to the tent. Odysseus and I rushed over.

"I'm sorry, I don't see your name on the list," a guard was saying to a small, curly-haired woman.

"I just want to look," the woman whined, and as she spoke, she drew back her arm and threw a fist-sized object into the throng of wedding guests.

Odysseus and I both tensed up, half expecting the thing to hit a wedding guest in the head. But it landed on the ground with a harmless thud.

The woman turned, and I saw her face. It was Eris! Eris, the uninvited. Eris, the angry. Eris, the troublemaker. Her eyes met mine, and she broke into a jagged smile.

"They'll be sorry they left me out, Hades!" she screeched. Then she whirled away from the guards and vanished into the night.

A mortal wedding guest had picked up

whatever Eris had thrown, and a crowd had gathered around him. Odysseus and I hurried over.

"It looks like an apple," Odysseus said.

I nodded. "A golden apple."

"Something's written on it," exclaimed the wedding guest. "It says, 'For the fairest.'"

"Oh, then it's meant for me!" cried Hera, Queen of the gods, rushing over.

Gray-eyed Athena, goddess of wisdom and war, was hot on her heels. "No, no, it's for me!" she said.

Golden-haired Aphrodite shoved in close to the wedding guest.

"*Caro mio*, my dear!" she said, sprinkling her unique version of broken Italian into her conversation as always. "Give the apple here."

"Oh, brother," Odysseus muttered.

The wedding guest looked puzzled. "Maybe I should keep it," he said.

"*La mia!*" cried Aphrodite, grabbing the apple from his hand. "Is mine!"

Athena snatched the apple from Aphrodite.

Then Hera plucked it away. After that, it was mayhem. Athena pulled Hera's hair. Hera kicked her in the shin. Aphrodite took a running start and head-butted Athena.

"Ohhhh!" Aphrodite moaned, holding her forehead. "You and your *stupido* helmet!"

Things went downhill from there. Those three goddesses fought over that golden apple like three dogs snarling over a bone. Things got so ugly that the wedding guests began to flee the reception. I saw Menelaus leading Helen away.

"Don't go!" cried Peleus.

"Don't you want your party bags?" Thetis called after the departing guests.

Finally Zeus made his way over to the brawling goddesses. "STOP!" he bellowed.

The goddesses stopped fighting and untangled themselves. Hera's ear was ichoring, Aphrodite was missing some teeth, and Athena had two black eyes.

"Give me the apple," growled Zeus.

Hera reluctantly plunked it into his outstretched hand.

"Now back off!" snarled Zeus. "All of you. I don't want ichor all over my tux."

"I'm the fairest, aren't I , Zeusie, honey?" Hera asked her husband.

"Well, um . . ." Zeus stammered.

"Daddy!" Athena cried. "You know I'm fairest!"

"Uhhhh . . ." said Zeus.

"*Caro Jupiter*!" crooned Aphrodite. "Dear Zeus! Who is the goddess of *amour* and *bellezza*? Love and beauty? It's *me*!"

Zeus looked around frantically. I could almost hear his brain whirring as he tried to come up with a way to get out of picking one of them. Finally, he shouted, "A mortal shall choose who's fairest!"

This is it, mortal readers. Zeus's cowardly act! Remember I said I'd tell you all about it? Well, here it goes.

If Zeus had only stepped up and named one of the goddesses as the fairest, the other two goddesses would have been hopping mad. They might have cried and sulked and pouted or planned some sort of petty revenge, but before long, it would have been forgotten. But no. Zeus had to go and drag a mortal into the mess. And *THAT* is where the trouble started.

"A mortal?" cried Hera.

"What do mortals know?" exclaimed Athena.

"A handsome mortal man?" asked Aphrodite. "*Molto bello?*"

"Yes, yes," Zeus said. "As handsome as they come!"

"Who? Who?" cried the three goddesses.

Zeus was thinking so hard that drosis — god sweat — broke out on his brow. At last he shouted, "I'll let you know! Until then, no more fighting. Got it?"

The three nodded unhappily.

"Now go find some nectar and ambrosia and fix yourselves up," he added. "Not one of you looks fair right now."

The three goddesses shrieked and scurried away to make repairs. Zeus stuck his cigar back between his teeth, pocketed the apple and stomped off.

"This isn't going to end well," Odysseus said, shaking his head.

"It sure isn't," I agreed. But back then, I didn't have a clue how much trouble Zeus was about to stir up.

CHAPTER IV

A DIP IN THE STYX

I know how Zeus thinks. He was hoping that if he stalled long enough coming up with a mortal to judge the fairest goddess, Hera, Athena, and Aphrodite would just forget about the whole thing.

Fat chance.

Still, Zeus's stalling meant that he'd lie low for a while, and I wouldn't have to worry about him. That left me free to spend time in the Underworld.

One morning, while Persephone was up on

earth, I went patrolling beside the River Styx. Harley and Davidson were trotting along at a nice clip, and Cerbie was riding shotgun. Charon was polling a few new ghosts over to my kingdom in his River Taxi. In short, everything was as it should be.

But suddenly, Cerbie lifted his heads. All six of his ears pricked up, and he started whimpering in triplicate. The only time I'd ever heard him whimper like that was when baby Perseus was around.

"What is it, Cerbie?" I asked. "You hear something?"

And then I heard it, too — a baby, bawling its head off.

Cerbie jumped to the floor of the chariot and squeezed himself under the passenger seat. Baby Perseus had scarred him for life.

As I rounded a bend, the crying grew louder. On the other side of the river, I spotted a woman wading into the Styx. She was holding a baby.

"Giddy-up, steeds!" I cried, racing toward the River Taxi. I sped onto it, giving Charon two gold coins — double the normal fare — to get me across, fast!

I knew what was going on. The waters of the River Styx can make a mortal invincible. Knowing that, you'd think mortals would be lining up day and night to take a plunge into the Styx, right?

Wrong.

First of all, unless you know my shortcut, it takes nine days and nights to travel down to my kingdom. Second, the River Styx is dark, sluggish, and cold as ice. Nothing could possibly live in its thick, foul-smelling waters, and yet creatures slither about under the surface, creatures with fangs and claws. Just thinking about them gives me the willies, and it's my river.

As soon as we reached the other side, I cried, "Giddy-up, Harley! Giddy-up, Davidson!" and I raced toward the wader. As my chariot drew near, I spotted a beach towel on the bank of the Styx. That was a first.

As I slowed my steeds, I saw the woman turn the screaming baby upside down. Holding it by a heel, she dipped the baby into the river and pulled it out.

"Enough!" I shouted. "No mortal can survive a second dip!"

The woman looked up.

"Thetis!" I cried.

"Hello, Hades." The sea goddess smiled at me. Holding the crying baby above the water, she waded to the shore.

I jumped out of my chariot. Normally, Cerbie jumps out with me, but his fear of babies is greater than his loyalty to me, and so he stayed where he was, cowering under the seat.

"This is my son, Achilles," Thetis said, drying him and wrapping him in the towel.

"A son!" I exclaimed. "Already? But you and Peleus were just married."

"We've been married for years, Hades," Thetis said.

"I lose track of time down here," I mumbled.

"Achilles is mortal, like his father," Thetis went on. "A seer told me that my son is fated to die in battle."

I shook my head. "A sad prophecy indeed," I said.

"One I'm hoping to change," Thetis declared. "I came here to make him invincible." She hugged Achilles close. "If something is fated to happen, it happens," she added. "I know that. But now Achilles is impenetrable to steel. Perhaps this will protect him in many a battle, and he can live to a fine old age."

"I hope so," I told her.

Thetis told me she'd walked for nine days and nine nights to reach the River Styx. I figured the least I could do was to give her a ride home.

Thetis climbed into my chariot with Achilles. As I drove toward the shortcut back to earth, the baby started crying again. Cerbie wrenched himself out from under the front seat of my chariot, leaped to the ground, and raced for the River Taxi as fast as he could go.

* * *

I dropped off Thetis and her son and decided

to check on Persephone to see how spring was coming along.

"Hades!" she exclaimed when she opened the door of her little apartment in Athens and saw me standing there. "What a nice surprise!"

She had only a few minutes before she was due in the olive groves, but we sat down in her living room and I told her about Thetis and Achilles.

"Poor Thetis, married to a mortal," Persephone said with a sigh.

"It must be hard," I agreed. "So, what on earth is new, P-phone?"

"The apple blossoms are coming along nicely," she told me. "And the almond trees are leafing out like crazy."

I half listened to Persephone telling me about spring. The other half of my brain was wondering, *Who's on the program tonight at Wrestle Dome?* Maybe I'd stop by and catch a match.

"Oh, and get this, Hades," said Persephone. "Zeus finally came up with a mortal to judge which goddess is the fairest."

That got my attention. "Who?" I asked.

"Paris," said Persephone.

"Who?" I'd never heard of the guy.

"He's a shepherd," Persephone said. "He has a flock of sheep up on Mount Ida."

"Zeus picked a *shepherd*?" I said. "Who told you that?"

"Artemis," said Persephone. "She saw him when she was out hunting. She says he's so good-looking that all the girls from nearby villages visit him on the mountainside and stitch fancy robes for him to wear while he tends his sheep."

"A shepherd who likes fancy clothes?" I frowned. Something wasn't right here.

Persephone shrugged. "Artemis says Paris is a good archer, and he's drop-dead handsome," she went on. "But . . . he's not all that bright."

"Ah." Now I understood. Any mortal with half a brain would find a way to wriggle out of agreeing to judge three powerful goddesses, because no good could come of it. No good at all. Zeus had picked Paris because he was dumb enough to go along with his scheme.

"Hermes is flying to Mount Ida tomorrow to deliver the golden apple," Persephone went on. "He'll tell Paris what he has to do and then the goddesses will arrive. Listen, Hades, I have to run. If those trees don't bear olives soon, Greece won't have any olive oil."

"Go on, Phoney, honey," I told her. "I'll let myself out."

I intended to go right back to the Underworld, but instead I found myself making a turn into the Athens Chariot Garage.

"I'll be back in a few days," I told the attendant when I dropped off Harley and Davidson. "Take good care of my steeds."

If we major gods and goddesses want to go somewhere — anywhere, really — we astro-travel. We do it by chanting a *ZIP!* code, and *ZZZZZIP!* Instantly, we're there.

I headed straight from the garage — *ZZZZZIP!* — to Wrestle Dome. Perfect timing! I hadn't missed a minute of the match. I took a seat in the god section and cheered for Eagle-Eye, who was up against Argus the All-Seeing. Argus has a *hundred* eyes, and yet Eagle-Eye Cyclops, the one-eyed wonder, won!

* * *

Early the next morning, I put on my Helmet of Darkness — *POOF!* — and *ZZZZIPPED!* over to Mount Ida. I wanted to see for myself which goddess Paris the shepherd would judge as the fairest.

I landed in a sheep-filled meadow. Below, at the base of Mount Ida, I could see the tall stone walls surrounding the city of Troy.

Stepping carefully, I made my invisible way through the sheep toward a handsome young mortal with golden curls and skin bronzed from the sun. A real looker! He wore a fine blue robe with gold and silver stitching. He was talking to Hermes.

"It's not that complicated, Paris," Hermes was saying. "Three goddesses are going to show up. You pick the one you think is the fairest and give her the golden apple."

Paris scratched his head. "But how will I know which one to pick?"

"Use your eyes!" said Hermes. "You're the judge. Whoever you think is prettiest gets the apple, okay?"

"Okay." Paris nodded. "Hey, how do I look?"

"It's not about you!" Hermes snapped, fluttering the little wings on his sandals impatiently. "It's about the fairest goddess."

"I know," said Paris. "But I want them to see how handsome I am."

"They'll see! They'll see!" Hermes spread his little wings, flapped up over Paris's head, and began circling him. "Now tell me what you're going to do when Hera, Athena, and Aphrodite show up."

"I'm going to give the pretty one the apple," said Paris.

"Right," said Hermes. He swooped down and dropped the golden apple into Paris's hand. "Good luck!"

As I watched Hermes flutter out of sight, a golden glow appeared in the eastern sky. No wonder the little messenger god was so eager to make a quick retreat — the goddesses were on their way.

The glow grew bigger and brighter, until out of it stepped three gorgeous goddesses.

"Wow, wow, wow!" said Paris.

I sat down on the hillside to watch the show.

"Greetings, Paris!" said Hera, smiling radiantly. "I am Hera, Queen of the gods and goddess of marriage."

"Good wishes, Paris!" said Athena. "I am Athena, goddess of wisdom and war." She flashed a smile as bright as her silvery helmet.

"Paris, *caro mio!*" said Aphrodite. "I am Aphrodite, goddess of *amore*, love, and *bellezza*, beauty." She tilted her head and blinked her eyes at Paris.

"I'm the fairest," Hera cut in. "Just give me the golden apple."

Paris held the apple out to her.

"Hold it!" Athena cried. "Take a closer look at me!" She stepped toward Paris, and he offered her the apple.

"Wait!" cried Aphrodite. "I'm goddess of *bellezza*! The apple belongs to me!"

"Here." Paris held out the apple. "Take it."

"Paris!" snapped Hera. "You're supposed to judge which of us is fairest and give the apple to that one. Got it?"

I smiled. Hera couldn't stop being bossy even when it might hurt her chances for a golden apple.

"But you're *all* so beautiful," Paris protested. "I can't decide."

"Let me help you," said wise Athena. "Pick me, and I will make you a great general. You will be a leader of armies!"

Paris's eyes lit up. "I'd get to wear a uniform!" he said.

"Wouldn't you rather wear a golden crown, Paris?" offered Hera. "Choose me, and I will make you king of many lands!"

"A king!" said Paris. "With purple robes!"

"*Caro mio!*" crooned Aphrodite. "Give the apple here and for a wife, I will give you *la donna piu bella nel mondo*!"

"Huh?" said Paris.

"You shall marry," said Aphrodite, "the most beautiful woman in the world."

"Deal!" Paris handed Aphrodite the golden apple.

Aphrodite smiled. "Oh, *caro mio*!" she said. "You won't be sorry!"

"Oh, yes, he will," growled Hera.

"Super sorry," hissed Athena.

"Who is the most beautiful woman in the world, anyway?" Paris asked.

"Helen of Sparta," said Aphrodite.

"Wait!" cried Hera. "Helen is already married to King Menelaus."

Aphrodite shrugged. "All will work out."

"This is so unfair!" sniffed Athena.

"This is bribery!" said Hera.

ZZZZZZIP! ZZZZZZIP!

The two angry goddesses vanished from Mount Ida.

Aphrodite turned to Paris. "Guess what, *caro mio*?" she said. "Your father is the king of Troy."

This was news to me.

"No wonder I like to wear fancy robes," said Paris. Then he frowned. "But, if he's the king, then what am I doing out here in the middle of nowhere, tending sheep?"

"Some old prophecy." Aphrodite waved her hand, as if to say it meant nothing. "Just before you were born, *tu madre*, your mother, have a dream and wake up screaming that Troy is burning. *Tu padre*, your father, call in the seers to say what the dream means. They say that baby about to be born will bring ruin to Troy. So when you born, your *padre* sends you here."

"Wow," said Paris.

"It is all so long ago, *caro mio!*" Aphrodite smiled.

I felt like shaking the goddess of L & B! Where did she get off saying that to Paris? She should know better than to mess with a prophecy.

"Here's what you do, *caro mio*," Aphrodite went on. "Go to Troy. Tell your *padre* who you are and have him set you up with a ship. Then sail to Sparta, get Helen, and bring her back to Troy."

"Will she want to come with me?" asked Paris.

"Si, *caro mio*," said Aphrodite. "She will."

"Which way is Troy?" asked Paris.

"You see it?" Aphrodite pointed, and Paris took off down the mountain.

"Baaaaaaa, baaaaaaaaaaaa!" his sheep called after him, but Paris just kept on walking.

CHAPTER V

GO BACK! GO BACK!

Hidden by my Helmet of Darkness, I stuck
with Paris as he made his way to Troy. When
he reached the city, he looked up and said,
"Awesome!"

He had that right. Troy was an amazing sight.
Set into the mountain, the great walled city faced
a wide plain that sloped down to the sea.

Paris cupped his hands to his mouth and
called, "Hello, up there!"

A guard appeared on the wall. "What do you
want?"

"I am Paris!" said Paris. "My father is the king. Let me in!"

The guard disappeared. Moments later the massive wooden gates of Troy swung open, and an old man walked out.

"Paris?" he said. "Is that you?"

"Yes!" said Paris. "Now take me to my father, the king!"

"I am King Priam," the old man said. "Welcome home, my son!"

Paris hurried to meet his father, and they walked into the city together. I was right on their heels. The big wooden gates immediately banged shut behind us.

King Priam put an arm around his son. "You're very handsome, my boy," he said "Come! You must meet your brothers. Well, not all fifty of them at once."

Paris was getting the royal welcome. Had Aphrodite clouded King Priam's mind, making him forget about the prophecy?

"Ah!" said King Priam. "Here comes one of your brothers now."

Striding toward them came a tall, broad-shouldered man with dark curls and blue eyes. He smiled broadly and said, "Greetings, my father!"

"Greetings, Hector," said King Priam. "This is your brother, Paris, home from Mount Ida."

"Welcome home, Paris!" Hector said. He clapped his brother on the back and continued on his way.

Paris turned to King Priam. "Father, can you set me up with a ship so that I can sail to Sparta?"

I figured Priam would tell Paris that he'd only just arrived, that he shouldn't sail off so quickly.

But Priam said, "Of course, my boy. I'm so happy you're home, I'll give you whatever you want."

My heart sank.

"You shall have a house with a courtyard on my palace grounds, just like all your brothers," King Priam went on. "Come! Let's get you some food. You must be hungry after your long journey."

"I am!" said Paris.

I was hungry, too, so I tagged invisibly along to the palace kitchen. When the servants were busy welcoming Paris, I snagged some stuffed grape leaves and a nice piece of baklava, sprinkled on some Ambro-salts, which I always carry in my wallet, and turned it into a snack fit for a god.

* * *

Word of Paris's arrival spread through Troy. Many of his brothers came to greet him. So did one of his sisters, Cassandra.

Poor Cassandra. When she became a priestess at Apollo's temple, Apollo gave her the gift of prophecy. But years later, she decided to stop being a priestess and get married. Apollo was so angry that he put a curse on her. Cassandra could still tell the future, but nobody would believe her.

Cassandra found Paris sitting on top of the Trojan wall, looking out at the seashore where

King Priam was arranging for his ship. I hovered nearby.

"Greetings, Paris," Cassandra said, sitting down beside her brother on the wall. "Is it true that you wish to sail off to capture Helen, Queen of Sparta?"

"That's right," said Paris.

"If you do this, doom will come to Troy," Cassandra told him.

"Don't be such a downer," said Paris.

"Believe what I say!" cried Cassandra. "I have the gift of prophecy."

"Oh, right," said Paris. "And I have two heads."

"If you steal Helen," said Cassandra, "Troy will end in ruins!"

"Buzz off," said Paris.

* * *

A few nights later, Trojan soldiers invited Paris to their campfire. As the fire burned down, their leader spoke.

"Paris," he said, "do not go to Sparta to steal Queen Helen."

"I'm going," said Paris.

"Your sister Cassandra says that if you kidnap Helen, a terrible tragedy will befall Troy," another soldier said.

"You believe her?" asked Paris.

"Well . . . no," the soldier admitted. "But other seers say it, too. Don't go!"

"Oh, what's the worst that could happen?" said Paris.

"We know not!" wailed a third soldier. "We only know it will end badly."

"I'm going," said Paris. "Helen and I are meant for each other."

And when his ship was ready, Paris sailed for Sparta.

* * *

ZZZZZZIP! I astro-traveled to the palace in Sparta to warn Helen. I made my way down tapestry-covered hallways, thinking that if Helen were truly fated to run off with Paris, there was nothing I could do to stop her.

But was it her fate? I wasn't so sure.

None of the seers had said *WHEN* Helen runs off with Paris, terrible things *WILL* happen. The prophecies were more like warnings. *IF* Paris takes Helen to Troy, *THEN* it will end badly.

That *IF* kept me working to stop it from happening.

I poked my head into the Loom Room.

"Hades!" Helen exclaimed when she saw me. "This is quite the day for visitors. My sister Clytemnestra just arrived from Mycenea with her children, and now you show up!"

She turned to a small girl sitting beside her, weaving on her own little handloom. "Hermione, say hello to King Hades."

"Hello," said Hermione. She was a pretty child, even if she did look really uncomfortable in what appeared to be a heavy, itchy tapestry dress.

"I need to speak with you, Helen," I said.

Helen got the message. "Hermione?" she said.

"Go find Aunt Clytemnestra and play with your cousins."

Hermione tossed her loom onto the floor and dashed from the room.

"She doesn't seem to like weaving," Helen said, sending her shuttle flying through the threads of her loom. "Isn't that odd?"

"Helen, I need you to promise me something," I said, taking a seat on a tapestry-covered couch. "Promise me you'll always stay in Sparta with Menelaus, no matter what."

"I'm Helen of Sparta," Helen said. "Menelaus and I are happy together, and Sparta has always been my home. Why would I ever leave?"

"Many men admire your beauty," I told her. "One might try to steal you away."

"Oh, beauty schmooty." Helen made a face, and even then she was the most beautiful woman in the world.

* * *

I longed to get back to the Underworld. With

assistants as old and slow-moving as Hypnos, the god of sleep, and Thanatos, the god of death, I knew there wasn't much getting done in my absence. And I missed Persephone. I missed my pooch. But I stayed in Sparta, hoping to head off disaster.

And one day I spied a Trojan ship sailing up the river. Paris stood on the bow, a leopard skin draped over his shoulders. He wore a wide gold belt and a pair of knee-high golden sandals. I had to give it to the guy — he was a snappy dresser.

As King of Sparta, Menelaus went to the dock to meet the ship.

"Welcome to Sparta, stranger!" he called. "Do you come in peace?"

"That's right!" called Paris. "I am Prince Paris of Troy, and I have come to . . . um, talk to you about how Troy and Sparta can . . . uh . . . cooperate!"

"On what?" said Menelaus.

"Oh, you know," said Paris. "Work together."

Menelaus looked a little unsure, but he said,

"Tonight we shall feast in your honor, Prince Paris."

Menelaus didn't have a clue that the little swine had come to steal his wife.

I hung invisibly around the palace and saw how, night after night, Menelaus's servants poured wine into a golden cup for Paris. Night after night, Paris feasted on roasted meats, breads, cheeses, and figs at Menelaus's table. And night after night, behind Menelaus's back, Paris winked at Helen, who wisely ignored him.

Paris had been in Sparta for several days when Menelaus received word that his uncle had died.

"I must go to my uncle's funeral," Menelaus told Paris at dinner that night. "I'll be back in a few days."

"Have fun!" said Paris.

"At a funeral?" said Menelaus.

Paris smiled. "Don't worry about a thing," he said.

The minute Menelaus sailed off, I headed for the Loom Room to keep invisible watch on

Helen. No way was I letting that sneaky Paris get anywhere near her!

Menelaus's ship was hardly out of sight when I heard voices outside the palace.

"Hurry, *caro mio*!"

"Don't rush me, man!"

I ran to the window. There was Paris, rushing toward the palace. Aphrodite and Cupid were right behind him!

"Helen?" I whispered.

"Who's there?" cried Helen.

"It's me, Hades," I said. "You can't see me, but I'm beside you. You need to come with me *now*!"

"Wait," said Helen. "I'm almost finished with this new robe for Hermione."

"Emergency! Can't wait!" I cried as Cupid darted into the room.

ZING!

"Ouch!" cried Helen. "I'm stung!"

Cupid dashed out the door, and Paris ran in.

Helen looked up at him. "Well, hello!" she said, smiling so brightly I wished I were wearing my god shades. "Am I ever happy to see you!"

"Yeah?" said Paris. "Happy enough to sail away with me and become Helen of Troy?"

Helen sighed happily. "Of course."

"Awright!" Paris grinned. "Let's hit the road, Helen!"

"I'll just throw a few things into a bag, sweetie," said Helen.

Sweetie? I'd never felt so helpless!

Helen rushed from the Loom Room, calling to her servants, "Bundle up my wool! Pack my spindle and loom! We're going to Troy!"

I took off after her. Maybe I could lock her up somewhere in the palace until Cupid's love potion wore off.

But Helen ran to her bedroom, where she was surrounded by fluttering attendants. There was no way I could whisk her off to a hiding place.

Right then a terrible thought hit me. What if Cupid had shot Helen with a red Love-Eternal arrow? The one that *never* wore off?

I found the little stinker in the kitchen, eyeing a platter of cabbage rolls.

I whipped off my Helmet.

FOOP!

"Zowie!" cried Cupid. "You scared the ichor out of me, Hades!" He tried to catch his breath. "What's wrong with you, man? You're all red in the face."

"You're what's wrong with me, Cupid!" I shouted. "Why did you zing Helen?"

"Mom made me do it," whined Cupid. "And Zeus. He's crazy about Paris. What was I supposed to do, say no?"

"Try it some time!" I glowered at him. "What kind of arrow did you use? The yellow Kiss-Me-Quick arrow? The orange Three-Day Special? Please tell me it wasn't a red one!"

"None of your beeswax, Hades," Cupid muttered.

"Tell me NOW!" I shouted.

"Jeez, man, calm down!" whimpered Cupid. "It's a new, pink-tipped arrow. I call it the Smoochie Woochie."

"Smoochie Woochie?" I didn't like the sound of that. "How long does it last?"

Cupid shrugged. "I don't know! It's an

experiment, man. I've never shot one before. Okay, I'm outta here, Hades."

He began chanting a *ZIP!* code, and before I could say another word, he was gone.

I jammed my Helmet back on — *POOF!* — and ran from the kitchen.

"Helen!" I called. If I could get to her before she boarded that ship, maybe I could talk some sense into her.

I ran to her bedroom, but Helen and all her servants were gone.

"Helen! Where are you?" I called again.

I checked the Loom Room. Empty.

I hurried to the window and saw Helen walking up the gangplank of Paris's ship. Behind her came a line of servants, carrying her trunks and all her weaving equipment. That girl did *not* travel lightly.

ZZZZZZIP!

I landed on the dock, but Paris's ship had just pulled out into the river.

I had to talk to Helen! Had to get her off that ship! The fate of Troy depended on it. And so, even though I can get seasick on Charon's River Taxi . . .

ZZZZZZIP!

I landed unseen on the deck of Paris's ship as it left the river and sailed out onto the open sea. At first the wind was brisk, and the ship sped through the waves. My godly stomach lurched a little while I searched for Helen, but it was nothing I couldn't handle.

I found her in a cabin near the bow of the ship. She was sitting next to Paris, knitting.

"These socks will keep your tootsie wootsies warm," Helen crooned, her needles clicking.

"Thank you, sweetsie weetsie!" said Paris.

My stomach lurched again, but this time it wasn't the sea making me sick. I tried everything I could think of to get Helen alone, but she never left Paris's side.

And then one day, the winds stopped blowing. A dead calm descended over the sea, and Paris's ship went nowhere. It rose and fell on every swell of the waves, rocking from side to side, and it made me sooooo sick! All I could do was hang over the ship's rail, which is where I was when I saw a large shape rising from beneath the sea.

"Sea monster!" shouted one of the crew as a huge shaggy head rose up from the waves.

Sailors screamed in terror, but I'd seen that head before. It belonged to Thetis's father.

"I AM NEREUS!" cried the Old Man of the Sea. "I COME WITH A MESSAGE FOR PARIS."

"Yeah?" said Paris.

"GO BACK!" cried Nereus.

"I'm not going back," said Paris. "Helen and I are sailing to Troy."

"GO BACK, I SAY!" cried Nereus. "IF YOU SAIL TO TROY WITH HELEN, A TERRIBLE TRAGEDY WILL BEFALL YOU AND ALL YOUR FAMILY. GO BACK!"

Paris turned to Helen. "Do you want to go back to Sparta, sweetie pie?"

"No!" said Helen. "I want to go to Troy with you, honeybunch."

Paris looked down at Nereus. "You heard the lady," he said. "We're not going back."

Nereus shook his shaggy head and sank back

down beneath the waves. Soon the winds began to blow again, and a few days later, we reached Troy.

Sick as a dog, I stumbled invisibly off Paris's ship. When my head stopped spinning, I looked around. The wide Trojan plain was filled with people holding signs saying, *Welcome, Helen of Troy! Welcome, World's Most Beautiful Woman!*

I groaned. In their excitement to welcome beautiful Helen, the Trojans seemed to have forgotten all about the prophecy!

Paris hooked his arm through Helen's. Together they walked down the ship's gangplank to the cheers of the Trojans.

"So, honey," purred Paris, "how does it feel to be Helen of Troy?"

"I love it!" Helen said, gazing up at the great walled city. "You know, sweetie, if I had a giant loom, I could make tapestries to hang on that wall."

"Anything you want, sugar," said Paris.

"Thank you, snookie wookums!" said Helen.

Ooooooh, I wanted to throttle Cupid for

shooting Helen with that vile Smoochie Woochie arrow!

I watched the giddy couple walk through the giant gates and vanish into Troy. The Trojan greeters followed, and the gates closed.

I stood outside the walls of Troy, invisible and alone. I'd failed in my mission to stop Helen from reaching Troy.

CHAPTER VI

THE OATH

I wondered how King Menelaus was taking the news that his wife had run off with Paris.

ZZZZZZIP!

I reached Sparta as Menelaus's ship pulled into the harbor. I saw that somewhere along the way, he'd picked up his friend, Odysseus.

Hermione ran down to the ship to meet her father. Clytemnestra and her children weren't far behind.

"Hi, Hermie!" Menelaus said, ruffling his daughter's hair. "Where's Mommy?"

"She sailed off with that weird guy who was visiting," Hermione said.

"What?" cried Menelaus. "You mean Paris?"

Clytemnestra nodded. "I'm sorry, Menelaus," she said. "Hermione speaks the truth."

"Paris stole Helen?" cried Odysseus.

Clytemnestra nodded again.

"Daddy, can I go stay with Aunt Clytemnestra until Mommy gets back?" Hermione asked. "Pretty please? She never makes me weave!"

"Fine, fine," Menelaus said, only half listening. He turned to Odysseus. "We must sail to Troy."

"Let's go, buddy," said Odysseus.

The two kings boarded Menelaus's ship. In no time, they were on their way to Troy.

I headed back to the Athens Chariot Garage. Was my bill ever a whopper! I hitched up Harley and Davidson and drove down to the Underworld to make sure everything was running smoothly.

It wasn't.

Hypnos had let the Pool of Forgetfulness spill over into the Pool of Memory. Now no one could remember which was which.

I'd ordered the ghost carpenters to put an

addition onto Motel Styx so I'd have room for new ghosts in case war broke out. But business was booming down at the Underworld Mall, and di Minos had hired away all the carpenters to build a huge complex he called Keroke for Korpses.

Worst of all, Cerbie was mad at me for staying away so long, and he'd chewed up the TV remote. He really knew how to hit me where it hurt!

When I finally patched up the remote and got it working again, I whistled for Cerbie to come into the den. But he trotted into the living room with Persephone.

"He thinks he's my dog now," Persephone said, stroking his heads.

"Cerbie, you're the guard dog of the Underworld," I reminded him. "Not the lap dog of the goddess of spring."

But Cerbie wouldn't even look at me, not with a single pair of eyes.

I barely got things straightened out before I had to rush back to Troy.

ZZZZZZIP!

I arrived to find Menelaus and Odysseus standing outside the city gates.

"Paris!" Menelaus shouted. "I've come to get Helen!"

"Show yourself, you dirty, rotten, sneaky, yellow-bellied lizard of a wife-stealer!" shouted Odysseus.

That mortal could really sling an insult.

At last Paris climbed up onto the wall and called, "Helen doesn't want to see you, Menelaus!"

"Liar!" shouted Menelaus.

"I'm not lying!" Paris shouted back. "Helen and I are in love. She wants to stay with me!"

Now Odysseus yelled, "Helen could never love a man wearing the hideous cloak you've got on, buddy!"

Paris gasped. "Helen wove me this cloak!" he cried.

"That's not his fault," Menelaus muttered as Paris jumped down from the wall and disappeared.

"How about challenging him to fight you?" said Odysseus. "You know, mano-a-mano."

Menelaus nodded. "I can take him."

Odysseus yelled out the challenge. "Come out, Paris, you stinking little weasel! Come out and fight Menelaus in hand-to-hand combat! The winner gets Helen."

Paris reappeared. He'd changed into a bright blue toga. At his side stood his brother, Hector.

"That sounds fair!" cried Hector.

"Very fair!" I shouted.

"Who said that?" asked Menelaus, looking around.

"Beats me," said Odysseus.

Oops!

"Are you coming out, Paris?" called Menelaus.

"Maybe," Paris called back.

Maybe sounded promising.

I *ZZZZZZIPED!* into Troy to make it happen.

"Fighting man to man is a noble thing to do," Hector was telling Paris when I arrived.

"He's really big," Paris said nervously.

"It's all that armor," said Hector.

I found Cassandra and sent her to talk to Paris.

"Send Helen back to Sparta with Menelaus!" Cassandra told Paris. "If she stays here, Troy will go up in flames!"

"Not that again!" Paris rolled his eyes.

"It's the truth!" said Cassandra. "Why don't you believe me?"

"Because everybody knows you're a liar, Sandy," said Paris.

Cassandra burst into tears. "You'll see!" she cried. "But by then, it will be too late!" With that, she ran off.

"Paris!" Menelaus called. "Come out and fight me like a man!"

But Paris kept stalling, so I sent some Trojan soldiers to talk him into the fight.

"If you fight him one-on-one," a soldier said, "then we won't have to fight a war."

"You're a soldier," said Paris. "Fighting's your job."

"*You're* the one who stole Helen," the soldier pointed out. "You should fight for her."

At last Paris jumped up on the wall. "All right, fine!" he shouted down to Menelaus. "I'll fight you tomorrow!"

I smiled invisibly as the Trojans cheered. Outside the wall, Menelaus and Odysseus high-fived. The one-on-one rumble was on!

* * *

Keeping my Helmet on, I made my way through Paris's house until I found Helen's weaving room. I arrived just as Paris was telling Helen that he'd be fighting Menelaus. When he left the room to talk to Hector, I wasted no time.

"Helen?" I said. "It's me, Hades." I removed my Helmet — *FOOP!*

"Hades!" cried Helen. "What are you doing here?"

"I came to see you," I told her.

"Me?" Helen looked surprised.

"Menelaus has come to get you, Helen," I said. "You have to go back to Sparta with him. That way, there won't be any trouble."

Helen giggled. "I can't go back," she said. "I'm Helen of Troy now. And besides, I love Paris."

"You think you do, but —"

I heard someone coming and clamped on my Helmet — *POOF!* — as Paris entered the room and threw himself down onto the couch.

"I didn't think Menelaus would come after you!" he wailed. "I don't want to fight him!"

"Poor schnookums!" said Helen. "Then don't!"

I groaned inwardly. This was hopeless! The one mortal who could stop the war had been taken prisoner by the Smoochie Woochie.

* * *

The day of the one-on-one fight dawned. Paris clanked out of his room dressed in three suits of bronze-and-leather armor.

"You're wearing all *that*?" said Hector when he saw him.

"I don't want to get hurt," said Paris.

Unseen, I trailed behind Paris as he made his

way to the gates of Troy. As he walked down a deserted hallway, a golden glow appeared and out stepped Aphrodite.

"No worry, *caro mio!*" she said. "I won't let him slay you."

"Don't let him wound me either, okay?" said Paris.

"Oh, *tesoro*, sweetheart." Aphrodite smiled. "I take care of you."

No, no, no, no, NO! I silently screamed as Aphrodite vanished. What was wrong with the goddess of L & B, anyway? Was her life so empty that she had to keep interfering in the lives of mortals?

Paris smiled. "Open the gates!" he called, and he clanked outside.

Paris approached Menelaus, and both men drew their swords. They began to circle one another.

Unused to wearing armor, Paris got his foot caught in his shin guard and tripped. Menelaus saw his chance and lunged! But Paris disappeared into a thick white mist.

Menelaus sliced at the mist with his sword. "Step out of that cloud and face me, Paris!" he shouted.

"You can't make me!" Paris taunted from inside the cloud.

Menelaus circled the mist. Every time he thought he saw Paris, he stabbed at him. But all he stabbed was air.

At last Menelaus shoved his sword back in its sheath. "Some immortal force is helping you, Paris!" he cried. "Against such a foe, I cannot fight."

Menelaus turned and stormed off toward his ship.

"Paris!" shouted Odysseus. "You're nothing but a low-down, no-good, lily-livered, chicken-hearted, cloud-wrapped coward!" He stomped off after Menelaus.

When he reached the ship, Menelaus turned toward the city. "Beware, Paris!" he shouted. "I shall return with many armies! I shall bring doom to Troy!"

The crew pulled up the anchor, and

Menelaus's ship sailed away. Only then did the cloud around Paris lift.

Paris grinned. "That wasn't so bad," he said.

It was all I could do not to throttle that boy! Not so bad? It was *terrible*! Paris wouldn't fight fair, one-on-one. So now there was going to be a war!

* * *

No way was I setting foot on a ship again, but when Menelaus and Odysseus arrived back in Sparta, I made sure to be there.

Menelaus went straight to Tyndareus, Helen's father, and told him what had happened. Tyndareus immediately sent messengers sailing to every Greek island in the Aegean Sea. His message was simple: Every Greek king must come to Sparta, *now!*

Soon the sea was filled with ships, and before long, kings filled the Spartan palace yard, just as they had when they'd come to woo Helen.

When every king had arrived, Tyndareus

stepped out onto the balcony — the very balcony where he had spoken to these men as suitors. Menelaus and his brother Agamemnon stood on either side of Tyndareus.

"Kings!" Tyndareus called. "Do you remember your oath?"

"Oath?" one of the kings said. "What oath?"

Menelaus spoke up. "When Tyndareus chose me to be Helen's husband," he said, "each of you swore an oath to obey me."

"Oh, *that* oath," the kings muttered.

"We swore it long ago!" called wise old Nestor.

"*Really* long ago!" called another king.

"An oath is an oath," said Tyndareus. "It doesn't have an expiration date."

"Prince Paris of Troy has stolen Helen!" Menelaus shouted to the crowd.

The kings gasped and shouted, "No! No!"

"Yes," said Menelaus. "And now I command every king to raise an army! I command every king to fight with me to win Helen back!"

A young man shouted, "Count me in!" He was big and strong, but way too young to have sworn that long-ago oath. "Let us sail for Troy and fight!"

"Achilles is right!" a king shouted.

Achilles? I did an invisible double take. Last time I'd seen Achilles, he'd been a screaming baby. And now, in what seemed the blink of an eye, he had great bulging muscles and stood taller than any man there. Here he was, grown and ready to fight for the Greeks. It made my head spin.

"No one wields a sword better than Achilles!" shouted a second king.

"Achilles can slay a lion with his bare hands!" a third king called.

"Achilles can run like the wind!" cried yet another. "Let us follow him into battle!"

I was amazed. Young Achilles was already a hero.

But not all the kings were so eager to fight.

"You were dipped into the River Styx, Achilles," wise old Nestor shouted. "You are invincible! But the rest of us are not so fortunate. We can die in battle."

"I can die, too!" Achilles shouted back. "My mother held me by the heel when she dipped me into the Styx. If someone shoots me in the heel, I'm a goner."

"What are the chances of *that* happening?" Agamemnon cried.

Achilles glared at Agamemnon. Agamemnon glared back. Anyone could see that these two strong-willed warriors didn't get along.

"An oath is an oath," Menelaus said. "The time has come for you to honor it. Return to your kingdoms, and raise your armies! Paint your ships black for war!"

"One year from now, we shall await you in Aulis Harbor!" called Agamemnon. "From there, we sail for Troy!"

All the kings cheered. Then Agamemnon and Odysseus, wise old Nestor and young Achilles, all bid each other farewell and sailed home to raise their armies.

CHAPTER VII

A THOUSAND SHIPS

Inspiration struck as I watched those kings sail away. Odysseus and Achilles were the most popular of all the Greek heroes. What if they never showed up at Aulis Harbor? The other kings and their armies would take that as a bad omen. They wouldn't want to go to war without their favorite heroes.

Some time later, I *ZIPPED!* to Ithaca to see Odysseus. I found him plowing a field with a sharp-bladed plow pulled by a pair of oxen.

"Odysseus, my man!" I called.

"Lord Hades!" he exclaimed, reining in his

team. "Telemachus!" he called to his young son, who was playing nearby. "Come say hello."

Telemachus ran over. "My father's told me about you," the boy said. "Do you really have a three-headed dog?"

I nodded. "Cerberus."

"I have a puppy named Argus," said Telemachus. "But he only has one head." He ran off to fetch the pup.

"Odysseus," I said, "don't sail off to fight Menelaus's battle."

"But I swore an oath to do so," Odysseus said.

"So easy to swear, but so hard to fight a war," I pointed out.

It took some convincing, but by the time I left him, Odysseus had decided to stay home.

Next, I visited Achilles's mother, Thetis. The sea goddess had found it difficult to live among mortals, so she had left Achilles with Peleus in Pithia and returned to her sea cave.

When I told her why I'd come, Thetis said, "Don't worry, Hades. Achilles is only fifteen. No way am I letting him go off to war."

"But how can you stop him?" I asked.

Thetis smiled. "Achilles has promised always, *always* to obey me," she said. "And so he shall."

* * *

The following year, black war ships began appearing in Aulis Harbor. Agamemnon and Menelaus kept a lookout for the ships of Odysseus and Achilles, but the ships never came. The kings and their men on the other ships began to grumble that if Odysseus and Achilles didn't come, they were going home.

My plan to stop the war was working!

But I hadn't counted on bull-headed Agamemnon. He was determined to have his great adventure in Troy. I soon learned that he'd sent his spy, Palamedes, to fetch the two heroes and bring them to Aulis.

I *ZZZZZZIPPED!* to Ithaca to warn Odysseus, and when Palamedes banged on the door of his palace, Odysseus and Penelope were ready.

"Where is King Odysseus?" Palamedes

demanded. "Agamemnon is waiting for him at Aulis Harbor."

"Poor Odysseus!" cried Penelope with tears in her eyes. "He's gone mad!"

"Is that right?" said Palamedes. He stormed out to the fields to see for himself, and there was Odysseus, plowing. The hero had long scraggly hair and a tangled beard. His little son Telemachus sat nearby, playing with his puppy.

"Planting my seeds, la, la, la!" Odysseus sang. But instead of seeds, he tossed salt into the plowed earth.

"So, you're a madman now, are you, Odysseus?" Palamedes called.

Odysseus just kept singing, "Tra la la la la!" and tossing more salt onto his field.

Without warning, Palamedes scooped up Telemachus and threw him directly into the path of the plow blade. Odysseus swerved to keep from running over his son.

"You're no madman, Odysseus!" sneered Palamedes. "Get your ships ready. You and your men sail for Aulis tomorrow."

Odysseus flashed him an angry look, and I thought that one day, Palamedes would regret tricking the great trickster, Odysseus.

Odysseus was going to war, but maybe I could still keep Achilles out of it.

ZZZZZZIP!

I arrived in Pithia and found Achilles in the town square. He was speaking to his father's great Myrmidon warriors, the fiercest fighters in all of Greece.

"We sail for Aulis tomorrow!" Achilles told them. "Then on to Troy, where we shall bring the Trojans to their knees!"

The Myrmidon warriors cheered.

Thetis had come out of her cave to spend time with her son, and now she appeared in the square. "Achilles!" she called. "Time to eat supper!"

Achilles rolled his eyes. "Be right back," he told the warriors.

I stuck invisibly with Thetis and Achilles as they made their way home.

"Sit down, Achilles," Thetis said when he

came inside. "You cannot go to war. You will be killed in battle."

Achilles sighed. "I'm invincible, Mom. Remember?"

"You never listen," Thetis said. "Here, put this on." She handed him a garment.

Achilles shook it out. "This is a woman's robe!" he cried.

"Put it on!" Thetis ordered. "I know what I'm doing."

Achilles groaned, but since he'd promised always, *always* to obey his mother, he put it on.

Thetis whisked Achilles off to the court of the king of Scyros.

ZZZZZZIP!

I stayed in Scyros long enough to see Thetis convince the king to let Achilles hide among his daughters. He had no beard yet, and in women's robes, with his muscles hidden, Achilles looked like a very large, very pretty girl. But one of the king's daughters was not fooled. Later I heard that this princess and Achilles were secretly married.

It took him a while, but Palamedes showed up in Scyros one day looking for Achilles. He roamed through the king's palace, snooping and sniffing. But Palamedes was fooled by Achilles's disguise, and he sailed back to Aulis without the hero.

I thought Achilles was safe. But just as I was about to *ZIP!* out of Scyros, Odysseus sailed in.

I yanked off my Helmet — *FOOP!* "What are you doing here?" I asked.

"If I have to fight," Odysseus said, "so does Achilles."

"But he's only a boy!" I said.

Odysseus looked me in the eye. "Achilles is a great young warrior of rare strength and power," he said. "The Greeks need him."

Then Odysseus began rubbing ashes into his beard to blacken it. Then he put on the robe of a traveling peddler.

"What are you doing?" I asked.

"Come and see," said Odysseus, slinging a pack onto his back.

POOF!

I followed him invisibly to the king's court.

"Hello, princesses!" Odysseus said, spreading out his wares. "Come! I have jewelry! Necklaces! Rings! Bracelets! I have a fine sword, too. But you ladies won't be interested in that."

The princesses, wearing veils to shield their faces from a stranger, ran out to see the peddler's goods.

"Look at this sparkly ring!" a princess exclaimed.

"Beaded bracelets!" cried another.

But one of the princesses had no interest in the glittering jewelry. She picked up the sword and tested the blade with her thumb.

"You like that sword, princess?" asked the peddler.

"No, no," said the princess in an odd, high voice, putting the sword down. "It's nice, but I'd rather have a dagger. I mean, a necklace!"

"Gotcha!" Odysseus cried, yanking off the veil covering Achilles's face. "You're going to war."

"Awright!" cheered Achilles, ripping off his women's garb. "My mom made me wear this stuff."

"I won't tell," said Odysseus. "Ready your ships, and tell your Myrmidon warriors that we sail tomorrow!"

Thetis cried to see him go. So did all the princesses. But Achilles? He couldn't have been happier.

* * *

My plan to stop the war was in shambles.

I chanted the *ZIP!* code for Aulis and arrived to find the great harbor filled with black war ships. Every ship was filled with Greek soldiers.

I caught sight of an old man in priestly robes boarding Agamemnon's ship. I moved invisibly closer to hear what he had to say.

"Oh, great Agamemnon!" said the priest. "I am Calchas, a seer from Troy."

"You're a spy!" said Agamemnon. "Be gone!"

"I am a seer," the priest said again, "and as I traveled here, I had a vision. I saw Greeks fighting a war with Troy!"

"That's no vision," said Agamemnon.

"Everyone knows that we Greeks are about to sail to Troy to fight a war."

"In my vision, the Greeks won the war," Calchas said.

"No kidding." Agamemnon smiled.

"No kidding," said Calchas. "So . . . I'm on your side now."

As Agamemnon welcomed Calchas onto his ship, I heard men cheering. I turned to see the twelve black ships of Odysseus sailing into the harbor. Right behind them came Achilles's ships filled with the Myrmidon fighting forces.

I looked out at Aulis harbor. There must have been a thousand ships waiting to sail for Troy. Was there any way I could stop them from sailing? It was no use asking for help from any gods or goddesses. Most of them had already taken sides in the war.

But I could ask Helen one more time. Surely when she saw a thousand black ships sailing into Troy, she'd understand that a terrible war was about to break out. I had to make her understand that only she could stop it!

I *ZZZZZZIPPED!* to Troy and found Trojan lookouts stationed in the high towers above the walled city. Their eyes scanned the sea for any sign of Greek ships.

Inside the walls, soldiers had gathered. Unseen, I walked among them. There was Hector sharpening his sword. There was Deiphobus, another of Priam's sons, trying on his shin guards. And there was Sarpedon, a mortal son of Zeus, mending his leather armor. But there was one Trojan prince I didn't see — Paris.

I hurried invisibly through the streets of Troy toward Paris's house. On the way, I passed a shrine holding the small wooden statue of Athena, known as the Palladium. The statue was said to have been dropped long ago from Mount Olympus. An old prophecy said that as long as the Palladium stood in Troy, the city could never be destroyed. No wonder priests stood guard over the statue.

When I reached Paris's house, I went straight to Helen's weaving room. I stepped in and removed my Helmet — *FOOP!*

"Hello, Helen," I said.

"Oh, Hades!" exclaimed Helen. "You always startle me." The years hadn't faded her beauty one bit. "I think of you and Persephone so often."

"Do you ever think of Menelaus?" I asked, getting right to the point.

She shrugged. "Sometimes."

"You and Menelaus were happy together," I said.

"And now I'm happy with Paris," said Helen. "Why are you asking me this?"

"Well, um . . . I'm wondering . . . do you think you'd be happy if you went back to Menelaus?" I was starting to drosis. Talking to a woman about her man problems was harder than I'd thought!

"I don't know, maybe," Helen said slowly. "I always loved the color of his hair."

"Great red hair," I said. "Amazing shade of red. And guess what? Menelaus is on his way here."

Helen's eyes grew wide and the shuttle slipped from her hand. "He's coming to see me?" she asked.

"It's a little more complicated than that,"
I told her. "Do you remember when you were
growing up in Sparta and your many suitors
filled the palace courtyard?"

"Sort of," said Helen. "It was a long time
ago."

"Do you remember," I went on, "that when
your father chose Menelaus as your husband, all
the other suitors swore that if any man stole you
away, they would all fight to help Menelaus win
you back?"

"Really?" said Helen.

"Really," I said. "And now the suitors are on
their way to Troy. The suitors and their armies."

"Armies?" said Helen. "Whatever for?"

"They're coming to fight a war over you," I
said.

"What?" cried Helen. "That's terrible!"

"Here's the good news," I said. "You can stop
the war!"

"How?" asked Helen. "I'll do anything!"

"Tell Paris that you want to go back to Sparta
with Menelaus," I said. "And when the Greek

ships reach Troy, send word to Menelaus that you'll go home with him."

Helen nodded. "I'll do it, Hades. I'll start packing up my yarns right now."

Yesssssss!

Just then Paris swept into the room wearing a tapestry cape and bright blue boots.

"Greetings, my little baklava," he said to Helen as he headed straight for her mirror. "Check the latest Paris fashion."

"Oh, honey!" exclaimed Helen. "You look like a million drachmas!"

Clearly, whenever Helen saw Paris, Cupid's Smoochie Woochie kicked in.

At last Paris turned away from the mirror and saw me. "Eek!" he screamed. "Who are *you*?"

"King Hades," I told him. The two of us were not on a first-name basis.

"Am I going to die?" squealed Paris.

"One day, yes," I said. "But that's not why I'm here."

"What a relief!" Paris put a hand to his chest. "I thought maybe I was going to die in the war that's about to start, but the truth is, I'm not going to fight."

"If there's a war," I said through clenched teeth, "it will be your fault."

"Not totally," said Paris. His eyes flitted back to his image in the mirror. "Stealing Helen wasn't my idea. Aphrodite told me to do it."

I turned to Helen. "Wasn't there something you were going to tell Paris?" I prompted her.

"Yes!" Helen broke into a smile. "I'm weaving you a brand-new pair of leggings!"

"Really, snookums?" cried Paris. "What color? Not red, I hope. Red would make my legs look fat."

I had to get out of there before I lost my lunch.

POOF!

ZZZZZZIP!

CHAPTER VIII
TAKING SIDES

I astro-traveled to a Greek warship to find out how close the fleet was to Troy. And how much time I had to stop this needless war.

The fleet was anchored near a deserted island. Some of the men had gone ashore. Wearing my Helmet of Darkness, I joined them so I could discover their plans.

"Look!" said one of the Greek kings as he stepped ashore. "There is an altar to Athena here."

"Let us make a sacrifice to Athena upon this altar!" said Philoctetes, the great archer, who always carried with him the Bow of Hercules and his poison-tipped arrows. "It will bring us luck!"

"Not so fast," warned Calchas. "First I must say the sacred rites."

"We have no time for that," said Philoctetes, and he quickly approached the altar.

"Stop!" cried Calchas. "I'm having a vision! I see that the altar is guarded by a vicious dog!"

As the seer spoke, a huge serpent darted out from under the altar and sank its fangs into Philoctetes's foot.

"I meant snake!" cried Calchas. "A vicious snake!"

"OW!" yelped Philoctetes. "OW! OW! OW!"

"Quiet!" said Calchas. "I need silence to say these rites."

But Philoctetes kept howling in pain. Some of the men carried him and his bow and arrows to a nearby cave. For days, they tried to treat the snakebite, but it turned into a horrible, foul-smelling wound. Nothing would heal it. Philoctetes howled and howled, "OW! OW! OW! OW! OW!"

The ships sat anchored by the island waiting for Philoctetes's smelly wound to heal. Around their campfires, the kings began to grumble.

"Is that foul wound a sign that the gods have turned against us?" one king wondered aloud.

"Maybe we should return home," another king said.

"I never knew a wound could stink *that* bad," muttered a third.

Odysseus heard their murmurings and went to Agamemnon. "If we stay here much longer, the men will revolt," he said.

"But we can't set sail with Philoctetes howling like that," Agamemnon said. "The Trojans will hear us coming from miles away. And on a ship we could never escape . . . that awful smell."

"I'll take care of it," Odysseus said.

That night, Odysseus gave Philoctetes an herb to make him sleep. He had his men put food and fresh water beside the poor man and rags for binding up his wound. Odysseus set the Bow of Hercules and the quiver of deadly arrows beside the sleeping archer. Then the Greeks snuck back to their ships. At dawn, they pulled up anchor and set sail for Troy, leaving poor Philoctetes behind.

I watched the ships sail off, thinking that Odysseus could be almost as slimy as my little brother Zeus.

The ships were sailing into the wind. I figured it would take them a week to get to Troy. That meant I had seven days to stop the war. Seven days to keep my Underworld kingdom from being overrun with way too many new ghosts!

Seven days wasn't much time. But a scheme was forming in my godly brain. One that could be carried out in only a few minutes.

I *ZZZZZZIPPED!* invisibly to Mount Olympus and headed straight to the Immortals' Archery Range, where I hoped to find the little god of love having target practice. And there he was.

I removed my Helmet. *FOOP!*

"YAHHHH!" cried Cupid, flinging his bow in the air and spilling arrows all over the place. "Why are you always doing that to me, man?"

"We need to talk, Cupid," I said.

Cupid groaned. "It's about the Smoochie Woochie, isn't it?"

I nodded. "It's been years since you shot Helen, and she's still as mushy as ever."

Cupid got down on all fours and began crawling around, picking up his arrows. "I told you it was an experiment," he muttered, stuffing the arrows back into his quiver.

"You know, Cupid," I said, "Your father Zeus has never really gotten over the time he fell in love with that Harpie."

"What?" Cupid looked up at me wide-eyed.

"Harpie," I said. "You know, the monster with a woman's head and the body of a chicken? The one that smells like rotten eggs?"

"Shut up, man!" cried Cupid, looking around nervously. "I don't need Dad finding out about that, okay?"

"You mean he doesn't know that you shot him with one of your . . ."

"No!" Cupid cut me off. "Don't even kid around about that, Hades."

I put my godly face close to his. "If you don't

want me telling Zeus why he was chasing after that Harpie, crowing like a rooster," I growled, "then you'd better do what I say."

"Okay! Okay!" cried Cupid. "What do you want me to do?"

"One week from today, meet me on the Trojan plain where the ships come in," I said.

Cupid nodded.

"I'll make sure Helen's there," I went on. "As soon as Menelaus steps off his ship, I want you to shoot Helen with a Forever arrow. *Forever!* Got that?"

"All right, I'll do it!" said Cupid. "But if my mom finds out about this, I'm toast."

* * *

As long as I was up on Mount Olympus, I figured I might as well see if I could talk any of my fellow immortals into calling it quits with the war.

I ran up the steps of the Great Hall and — what luck! Zeus had called some sort of meeting, and most of the Olympians were there, sitting on their thrones.

"Hades!" Hera said when I walked into the hall. "What now?"

"Nice to see you, too, Hera," I said. "Okay, listen up, Olympians!"

"Hold it, Hades," said Zeus. "I run the meetings up here."

"I just need to say a few words," I said.

"Make it quick," Zeus growled. He hated sharing the spotlight even for a second. What was the big hurry, anyway? He was immortal. He had all the time in the world.

"If Helen stays in Troy," I began, "there's going to be a terrible war between the Greeks and Trojans."

"*Vittoria* for Troy!" called out Aphrodite.

"No!" Athena argued. "Victory for the Greeks!"

"But Athena," I said, "your statue, the Palladium, is the protector of Troy! How can you be for the Greeks?"

"Oh, let's see, maybe it has something to

do with a certain Trojan prince," Athena said bitterly. "A certain rotten apple."

"Rotten is right." Hera snorted.

Great. Those goddesses were *still* fighting over that golden apple. I shouldn't have been surprised. Immortals love holding a grudge.

"Besides, I'm crazy about Odysseus," Athena said. "He's a smart one. As clever as they come."

Aphrodite turned to Ares, who was sitting beside her. "You will fight for Troy, *si, caro mio?*" she said.

"Sure," the god of war agreed. "Unless Troy starts winning. Then I'll help the Greeks. I'll do whatever it takes to keep the war going!"

Now Hephaestus, the god of the fiery forge and Aphrodite's long-suffering husband, spoke up. "If Aphrodite's for Troy " he boomed, "then I'm for the Greeks."

"I'm helping Troy," Apollo offered. "You should see the white marble temple those Trojans built for me. When it's sunny out, that place is so bright it practically blinds me, and I'm the god of light."

"Count me in for the Greeks!" shouted my blue-haired brother, Po, god of the seas. "Those guys are real sailors. Not like the Trojans who stay walled up in that dry-land city."

"You're rooting for the wrong team, Po," said Zeus. "My son Sarpedon is fighting for Troy. And take a look at Hector. He's strong and full of fight. Plus he's a hit with the ladies." He waggled his eyebrows. "Reminds me of myself when I was a young thunder god."

This was *not* what I was hoping to hear!

"Let me get this straight," I said. "If there's a war, some of you plan to help the Trojans. . . . "

"*Si!*" called Aphrodite.

"For now," Ares said.

"Yep!" said Apollo.

"You bet!" shouted Zeus.

". . . and the rest of you will help the Greeks," I finished.

"Right," said Hephaestus.

"All I can," said Hera.

"Me, too!" said Athena.

"You bet!" said Po.

"I forbid you to help the Greeks," roared Zeus.

"You can help Troy, but we can't help the Greeks?" cried Hera. "No fair!"

"Fair?" cried Zeus. "Who said anything about fair? I'm not even sure what it means."

For once, Zeus spoke the truth.

"But if you immortals help both sides, no one can win," I pointed out. "The war will go on and on and on!"

"So?" said Apollo.

"War is a great show," said Ares.

"And we've got so much time on our hands," said Athena.

I groaned. This war was nothing but a game to these gods and goddesses. Something to keep them entertained.

"But if thousands and thousands of new ghosts show up in the Underworld all at once, the place will turn into a great big howling mess!" I cried.

"*Caro mio*," said Aphrodite, "I care nothing for your kingdom."

"Me, neither, said Hera.

"Not at all," said Athena.

At least I'd gotten those three goddesses to agree on something.

Aphrodite rose from her throne and walked over to where there was a break in the clouds. "*Guarda!* Look!" she cried, peering down at the earth below. "Greek ships are almost to Troy!"

"What?" I cried.

We all ran over to look. Sure enough, those thousand ships were nearing the Trojan beach. The winds must have changed!

"I'll start things off!" Zeus cried. He reached into his Bucket o' Bolts, picked up a thunderbolt, and hurled it at the lead Greek ship. Well, *hurled* may be too strong a word. More like *tossed*.

I took off running for the Immortals' Archery Range. Cupid was still there.

"Now what?" he cried when he saw me coming.

"We have to go to Troy!" I said.

"But I need to —"

"NOW!" I cut him off. "You have a Forever arrow?"

"Yeah, yeah," Cupid muttered.

"Let's *ZIP!*" I said, and we did.

We hit ground outside the gates of Troy. A lookout in one of the towers was shouting, "Greek warships approaching! There must be fifty of them. No, wait, a hundred! No, wait . . ."

I put on my Helmet — *POOF!* — and hurried Cupid around the back of the city wall where he wouldn't be seen.

"Don't move!" I said. "I'll get Helen."

ZZZZZZIP!

Inside the walls of Troy, men hurried along the streets carrying swords, shields, and armor. Women and children ran every which way, shouting and calling. I headed straight for Paris's house and made my way to Helen's weaving room. It was empty.

"Helen?" I called.

A tangle of yarn spilled out of her silver basket, and her shuttle lay on the floor. It looked as if Helen had left in a hurry.

"Helen?" I called again as a golden glow appeared at the window. Before I could move a muscle, Aphrodite appeared and stepped out of the glow.

"Take off that *estupido* Helmet, Hades," she said. "I know you are there."

FOOP! "Listen, Aphrodite . . ." I began.

"No, you listen!" said Aphrodite. "I talk to my *Cupidino*. He tell me of your *estupido* scheme for his Forever arrow."

"You want to talk *estupido*?" I cried. "You had Cupid shoot Helen with that Smoochie Woochie. It's turned her into a mush pot!"

"What's done is done. *Finito!*" Aphrodite shrugged. "Helen is hiding away. You will never find her. And I send my *Cupidino* home."

I groaned. My plan had tanked!

"Give up, *caro mio*," Aphrodite said. "The war is about to begin."

CHAPTER IX
WAR!

ZZZZZZIP!

I touched down on the broad Trojan plain outside the city walls. The sea was thick with black ships speeding toward the shore.

Now the city gates opened. Troy's army poured out onto the plain. The warriors' war whoops filled the air as they raced toward the rapidly approaching Greek ships.

The first Greek ship nosed onto the sand. A warrior leapt onto the bow, waving his spear. No sooner had he shouted, "Now we take Troy!" than a Trojan arrow brought him down.

That didn't stop the Greeks. Hundreds of their soldiers — thousands of them! — leaped from their ships. Man after man came roaring at the Trojans. Swords clashed! Arrows whizzed through the air!

The Trojans fought mightily, but still the Greeks came, fighting and roaring and driving them back into their city. As the sun went down, not a single Trojan warrior was left on the plain.

As the Greeks gathered up their dead and began to make camp, I walked invisibly among them. Making my way through camp after camp, I saw Greek soldiers nailing together huts. They built shelters for the horses and cattle they'd picked up by raiding islands on the way to Troy. Other soldiers polished their brass-and-leather shields and sharpened their swords. Archers strung their bows. Stone slingers mended their wolf-skin shields.

I soon came upon Odysseus's camp. Like all soldiers, Odysseus fought barefoot, and I watched him trying on a pair of bronze-and-leather shin guards.

I passed the camps of many heroes, and in every one, men were hard at work preparing for war.

Finally, down by the sea, I reached Achilles's camp. The young hero sat in a folding chair, drinking a cup of wine while he watched his good friend Patroclus and the Myrmidon soldiers throwing the discus and javelin for sport.

Agamemnon had been surveying his troops, and now he stopped at Achilles's camp. "What's this?" he cried. "All prepare for war except the great Achilles?"

"I am prepared, Agamemnon," said Achilles, not getting up from his seat. "My Myrmidon forces know how to fight."

Agamemnon scowled down at Achilles. "See that you are ready for battle at sun up!" he said, stomping off.

* * *

At dawn the next day, the gates of Troy opened, and the Trojan cattlemen drove their herds outside to graze. Then the Trojan army swept out onto the plain. Whooping and shouting, the Greek forces ran to meet them.

Slingers from both sides threw stones. Archers shot arrows. In the thick of battle, I spotted red-haired Menelaus hurling his spear. Nearby, Odysseus was slashing his way through throngs of Trojans.

Now Hector strode through the gates of Troy, his bronze armor gleaming in the sun. With a great war cry, he charged into battle. Right on his heels came Zeus's mortal son, Sarpedon. All the Trojan heroes came roaring out to fight — except for Paris.

Ohhhh, it made my ichor run hot!

I stood there on the Trojan plain, listening to swords clashing and spears slamming into shields.

I hadn't stopped the war.

Now I had to get back to the Underworld ASAP and get ready for a population explosion.

ZZZZZZIP!

* * *

Weeks turned into months, and months into years, and still the war raged on. Every day, thousands of new ghosts flooded into my kingdom. Motel Styx was bursting at the seams.

And the ghosts? They were a messy lot, many of them missing body parts. Their moaning was horrible, but it wasn't about their wounds.

"Woe is us!" the new ghosts howled. "We died for beautiful Helen of Troy. And we never even got to see her!"

One morning I drove my chariot down to the River Styx as usual and steered my steeds onto the Charon's River Taxi.

"I'm making twenty times the usual number of trips each day, Lord Hades," Charon said as he poled me to the far shore of the Styx. "I need a vacation."

"You and me both, Charon," I muttered.

We reached the other shore just as Hermes's rusted-out old bus came clattering down to the riverbank.

I hopped out of my chariot as Hermes hit the brakes. He opened the bus door, and a load of Greek ghosts came floating out.

I frowned. Something wasn't right. These ghosts didn't look as if they'd been slain in battle. They looked sick and pale, even for ghosts.

"What battle did you die in?" I asked one of them.

"Noooooo battle," moaned the ghost. "Died of the plaaague!"

The plague? There's wasn't time to find out more. I had to keep these ghosts moving to make room for more ghosts.

"This way to the River Taxi!" I shouted.

When the bus was empty, Hermes jumped out. "Hades!" he said. "My tires are blowing every trip. You gotta get more buses! Hire more drivers!"

I nodded. Hermes was right.

Just then, two ghosts in the line started fighting. I rushed over.

"Break it up!" I told them. "Your fighting days are over."

"He says Agamemnon's too big for his britches," howled one ghost.

"He says Achilles thinks he's too cool for school," howled the other.

"But Agamemnon and Achilles are both Greeks," I said. "They fight on the same side. Your side! What's the problem?"

"We Greeks fall sicker by the day," moaned the first ghost.

"The seer Calchas says Apollo has sent a plague to punish us!" howled the second.

Sending a plague onto the Greeks? The god of light was showing his dark side.

"Calchas says Agamemnon can stop the plague by sacrificing something he loves to Apollo!" howled the first ghost. "But Agamemnon says Achilles must sacrifice something he loves, too."

"But Achilles said, 'No way!'" wailed the second ghost. "They had a terrible quarrel. Now Achilles won't fight for Agamemnon."

"What?" I cried. "Achilles is out of the action?'

Both ghosts nodded.

"Achilles sits in his camp and sulks," howled the first ghost.

"Agamemnon should apologize!" howled the second.

"Should not!" howled the first, and the two began fighting again.

I left them to it. I had to get up to Troy to find out what was happening.

ZZZZZZIP!

* * *

I arrived inside Helen's room fully visible.

"Oh!" cried Helen, dropping her golden yarn. "Hades!"

"Don't hurt me!" Paris screamed from where he stood in front of the mirror. He had the pelt of a huge black panther slung over one shoulder.

"Paris is getting ready to fight, Hades," said Helen.

"About time," I muttered.

Paris switched the panther pelt to the other

shoulder. "Is this better?" he asked, tilting his head and studying his reflection.

Footsteps sounded in the hallway. I ducked behind a screen as Hector raced in. "Paris!" he shouted. "Men are out there dying! And you prance around in front of a mirror? Come and fight!"

"I'm coming!" Paris grabbed two spears that were leaning against the wall. "I'll throw these. Will that make you happy?"

"Nothing you do makes me happy," Hector growled. He grabbed Paris by his panther pelt and dragged him from the room.

Helen smiled up at me. "Paris looks great in panther, doesn't he?"

"Not to me," I muttered, sorry to find Helen still suffering from the effects of the Smoochie Woochie. "Let's go out to the wall and watch the battle," I said, putting on my Helmet. *POOF!*

As we went, I asked Helen about Achilles and Agamemnon. She told me that after their quarrel, Achilles had refused to fight and had kept his friend Patroclus and his men out of the battle as well. Day after day, the Myrmidon warriors stayed in their camp, competing in games to see who could throw the discus or javelin the farthest.

We came to the spot where Trojan women and old men who could no longer fight sat on the wall, watching the battle. King Priam sat with them. He beckoned Helen to sit next to him. He seemed to understand that it had been Helen's fate to come to Troy with Paris, and he was kind to her.

Once Helen was seated, I whispered, "Be right back." And I *ZZZZZZIPPED!* down to the battlefield.

I didn't have to wait long before Paris, decked out in his panther pelt, strode through the gates of Troy. He held a spear in each hand. A bow was slung over one shoulder, and he had a quiver of arrows on his back.

"Look!" shouted one of the Trojan soldiers. "It's Prince Paris!"

A hush fell over the battlefield as Paris jogged past the Trojan troops. He wasn't even in throwing distance of the Greek army when he heaved his first spear. It fell harmlessly to the ground.

He was getting ready to throw the second spear when a Greek soldier charged out of the pack and ran at him, shouting, "Paris! Now is your time to die!"

It was Menelaus! He ran toward Paris as if he were a panther himself.

"Whoa!" cried Paris. He dropped his spear, turned, and ran swiftly back to the safety of Troy.

Hector stood inside the gates. "You coward!" he shouted at his brother. "You call that fighting?"

"The gods made you brave, Hector," whined Paris. "Don't hate me because the gods made me beautiful."

"What?!" cried Hector.

"Never mind." Paris sighed. "Okay, we can do that one-on-one thing again. The winner of the fight gets Helen."

"Do you mean it this time?" Hector asked.

Poor Helen. First her fate was decided by one

of Cupid's arrows. Now was it to be decided by a fight? Still, I was glad to see Paris nod. He meant it. Now maybe now this war would end!

"I'll let the men know," said Hector. "Stay here. I'll fetch you proper armor and a shield."

Hector hurried out to the battlefield to spread the word that Paris had agreed to one-to-one combat.

As soon as the news reached the Greeks, Menelaus shouted, "I shall fight Paris!"

The Greek warriors nodded. It was only right that Menelaus should fight for his wife.

One of the Trojan soldiers marked off a square on the plain as a fighting field. Warriors on both sides took off their armor and sat down, ready to watch the fight. It was starting to remind me of a match at Wrestle Dome!

I glanced up. Helen and Priam were still sitting on the wall and watching. And now I saw what godly eyes alone could see — Apollo, Aphrodite, Ares, and Zeus sat on the wall as well!

Ohhhh, I groaned. How I wished I could tell them, *Don't butt in!*

Wearing his borrowed armor, Paris walked once more through the gates of Troy. He stopped at the edge of the squared-off fighting field. Menelaus, decked out in his battle gear, stepped up to the opposite edge.

Hector wrote an *M* on one stone and a *P* on another. He put the stones into a helmet and shook them up. Closing his eyes, he reached in and picked a stone to see who would throw the first spear.

He picked the *P*.

Paris drew back his arm and threw a spear. It hit Menelaus's shield — *plonk!* — and landed on the ground.

Menelaus looked to the heavens. "Great Zeus!" he cried. "Give me victory over Paris, who came to my palace, ate my food, drank my wine, and stole my wife!"

I glanced up at Zeus sitting on the wall to see what he thought of Menelaus's plea, but he had his eyes on a young Trojan woman and wasn't paying any attention to the combat.

With a fierce cry, Menelaus hurled his spear. It

whizzed through the air, cutting through Paris's shield and armor. It stopped before it pierced his heart.

Now Menelaus drew his sword and rushed at Paris. He slammed the sword down on top of Paris's helmet so hard that the blade shattered.

With a furious roar, Menelaus grabbed the horsehair crest on Paris's helmet and began dragging him backwards. Paris yelped and screamed, and just as it looked as if his end was near, a golden glow appeared.

Back off, Aphrodite! I silently shouted.

But of course, she didn't. Unseen by mortals, Aphrodite cut the strap of Paris's helmet.

Menelaus staggered backward, clutching only the helmet in his hand. He tossed it into the throng of Greek warriors, and one of them threw back a sword. Menelaus leapt at Paris to finish him off — but he leapt into a cloud.

"Not again!" cried the furious Menelaus. "Show yourself, Paris! We must end this fight!"

Menelaus stormed and shouted, but it was no use. Aphrodite had whisked Paris away.

At last Menelaus shouted, "Helen is my wife! Bring her to me, and we Greeks shall sail for home!"

But the Trojans were as confused by Paris's vanishing act as the Greeks. And since Menelaus had not slain Paris, they were not going down in defeat.

"Helen stays in Troy!" cried a Trojan warrior, fastening on his armor.

"Helen goes to Greece!" cried a Greek warrior, picking up his shield.

And so the battle started up again, more fiercely than before. Greeks slew Trojans and Trojans slew Greeks, and all because the goddess of L & B couldn't leave well enough alone.

CHAPTER X
GHOST STORIES

Even down in the Underworld, I couldn't
escape the fighting. The place isn't soundproof,
you know. Horses thundered overhead, chariots
crashed, swords clashed. The noise was
deafening!

And when they weren't fighting, the Greeks
were piling up rocks and mud and sand to build
a huge earthen wall to protect their camps and
ships. In front of the wall they were digging a
trench so deep and so wide that no horse-drawn
chariot could cross it. They dug all night. Only
Hypnos could sleep through such a horrible
racket.

All that digging must have snapped some wires, because my cable was out. I couldn't even watch wrestling. I only hoped they'd be finished digging by the time Persephone came home for the winter!

One evening, I headed over to Motel Styx to see how my lieutenants were dealing with the overcrowding.

"Hypnos?" I called as I walked past the hundreds of tents pitched outside the motel. "Thanatos?"

I squeezed into the ghost-packed lobby of Motel Styx, and there, working the front desk, was Tisi.

"Hi, Hades," she said, flashing me a fang-filled smile.

Tisi's a Fury, one of three snake-haired, red-eyed, black-winged immortals who flies up to earth each night to hound the wicked and whip them with little scourges.

"Hypnos and Thanatos asked me to fill in here for the night," Tisi explained. "They had to go pick up the body of a Trojan warrior and take it home to be buried. One of Zeus's mortal sons, I think."

"Sarpedon?" I asked.

Tisi nodded. "He must be buried by now because his ghost just showed up."

"So I did!" wailed a ghost, and I recognized the shade of Sarpedon, the great Trojan hero.

"Tell us your tale!" howled the Trojan ghosts.

Sarpedon's ghost looked to me for permission.

"Why not?" I said. It would keep the ghosts entertained until we could find rooms for them all.

"The fighting was furious," Sarpedon's ghost began. "Agamemnon slew many of our fine Trojan warriors."

"All right!" cheered the Greek ghosts.

"Hector and I led more Trojan troops into battle," Sarpedon went on. "We chased the Greeks back to their ships."

"Go Troy!" shouted the Trojan ghosts.

"Then Odysseus charged us," said Sarpedon. "His forces pushed us until our backs were against the Trojan wall!"

"Go Greeks!" cried the Greek ghosts.

I went over and stood beside Tisi at the front desk, making a mental note to put a couple chairs back there.

"There was a break in the fighting," Sarpedon went on. "Hector went into the city of Troy to ask that an offering be made to Athena so that she might help us. When he came back to the battlefield, he told me that he'd found his brother Paris in Helen's chamber, playing with his bow and arrows as if they were toys."

"Helen! Helen!" cried all the ghosts. "Tell us about Helen!"

"Helen is so beautiful," Sarpedon said, "that all who see her fall in love with her."

"Oooooh," moaned the ghosts. For once, they agreed on something.

"When the fighting started up again, the Greeks took down many of our brave Trojan warriors," Sarpedon continued. "The Greeks would have slain more of us, but a sudden thunder bolt frightened their horses and caused them to run."

"Zeus threw a bolt?" Tisi whispered to me.

I nodded. Had to be Zeus.

"We fought on," Sarpedon said, "pushing the Greeks back to the great trench. Many of us jumped out of our chariots and crossed the trench on foot, but the mighty earthen wall stood before us. It was too high for us to climb over, so Hector picked up a boulder. It was enormous! No mortal man could have lifted it, yet Hector did."

"With a little help from Zeus," I whispered to Tisi.

She rattled her scourge angrily.

"Hector heaved the boulder at the wall, and it broke through," said Sarpedon. "We Trojans cheered, thinking victory was ours. But a mighty Greek warrior picked up another big boulder and threw it at Hector, smashing him to the ground. We thought he was dead, and then a white light appeared around our hero."

"White light?" whispered Tisi. "That's Apollo, right?"

I nodded. Why couldn't the gods leave the fighting to the warriors?

"When the white light faded, Hector leaped up, healed of his wounds," said Sarpedon. "He ran back into the battle, shouting to us to set fires. We lit torches and threw them onto the black ships. As the ships began to burn, who should appear but Achilles! He led the mighty Myrmidon warriors onto the field, and many a Trojan ran for his life."

"Did you run, Sarpedon?" a ghost called out.

"Never!" cried Sarpedon. "I galloped straight for Achilles, my sword held ready for the kill. But I was no match for him. Achilles slew me, and now . . . here I am."

Sarpedon had told a good tale. Some of the ghosts clapped, which didn't make any sound, but it was a nice gesture.

Now the ghost of a Greek warrior rose to his feet. "Achilles didn't kill you, Sarpedon!" he cried.

"He did!" exclaimed Sarpedon. "I recognized Achilles's armor!"

"It was Achilles's armor," the ghost agreed. "But I, Patroclus, wore it!"

"Tell your tale! Tell your tale!" chanted all the ghosts.

I gave a nod.

"I was in our camp with Achilles and the Myrmidons," Patroclus began. "The Greek forces were trapped with their backs to the ships. Night fell, and it became too dark for fighting, but in the distance, I saw campfires. I knew the Trojan warriors were only waiting for dawn to finish us off."

I leaned forward to listen. This was every bit as exciting as a wrestling match!

"Odysseus came to our camp to speak with Achilles," Patroclus went on. "I brought him food and wine, and listened to what he had to say."

"Tell us!" all the ghosts cried. "What did he say?"

"Odysseus said that King Agamemnon saw no way out for the Greeks," said Patroclus. "He was ready to tell warriors to sail back to Greece. But wise old Nestor spoke up. He said that if Achilles appeared on the battlefield, the Trojans would be so frightened that they'd run back into their city."

"True, true," murmured the Trojan ghosts.

"Odysseus asked Achilles to fight for the Greeks again," said Patroclus. "He said Agamemnon would give him gold and land back in Greece if he fought. Menelaus would give him his daughter Hermione for his wife."

"What did Achilles say?" called a ghost.

"He said no." Patroclus sighed. "The next day, the fighting began again. Reports came to our camp that Agamemnon and Menelaus had been wounded. And then I saw smoke coming from the Greek ships."

"We torched those ships!" Sarpedon cried.

"Shhhh!" said a Greek ghost. "You had your turn."

"I ran to Achilles," said Patroclus. "I begged him to fight, but he refused. So I asked him to give me his armor. I asked him to let me lead the Myrmidons into battle myself. He agreed and gave me his star-studded breastplate, his helmet, and his sword. Dressed in Achilles's armor, I climbed into his chariot and led his forces into battle."

"All right!" cried the Greek ghosts.

"The Trojans saw me and believed the great Achilles had joined the fight," Patroclus went on. "Every warrior, every hero, turned and ran for the safety of Troy! But I rode after them and cut them down like flies!"

"Hey, that's us you're talking about!" objected a Trojan ghost.

"Yeah, don't call us flies!" wailed another.

"It was I who slew you, Sarpedon!" cried Patroclus.

"So you did," replied Sarpedon. "And who slew you?"

Patroclus frowned. "We Greeks were sure that Hector was dead after being smashed with the boulder. But suddenly, there he was, back in the fight."

"Go Hector!" called a Trojan ghost.

"I heaved a stone at Hector myself, but it missed him," Patroclus went on. "He jumped out of his chariot and rushed at me. I drew my sword, but as I thrust it at him, the god Apollo appeared!"

"I saw this coming," Tisi muttered.

"Apollo knocked the sword from my hand," Patroclus went on. "He pulled the helmet from my head and then — only then! — did Hector slay me. The last thing I remember is him stripping off Achilles's armor."

Sarpedon sighed. "So, here we are."

"Yes," agreed Patroclus. "Here we are, and soon Hector will join us."

"Never will great Hector be slain!" cried Sarpedon.

"Oh, yes, he will," said Patroclus. "For when Achilles hears that I am dead, he will slay Hector."

Just then, Hypnos appeared and announced that he had fifty rooms available. All the ghosts quickly scrambled to their feet and ran off to claim one.

Tisi shook her head, waking up her snakes, which had been snoozing through the warriors' tales. "Helen must be a real looker to have caused all this trouble," she said, rattling her scourge.

"She's the most beautiful woman in the world," I said. "But don't even think about punishing her, Tisi. That poor mortal has suffered enough."

CHAPTER XI
ACHILLES'S ARMOR

Every time the Greeks came close to winning the war, some new hero would show up in Troy, saying he'd come to save the day, and the war would go on and on.

This sent an endless stream of new ghosts traveling down to my kingdom. Every square decameter of the Underworld was filled with howling, yowling, moaning, groaning ghosts. I had to put a stop to this war! It had gone on way too long.

I *ZIPPED!* up to Mount Olympus to have a talk with my fellow immortals. I found all the usual suspects hanging around the Great Hall. Zeus was there, too, snoozing on his throne.

"Zeus, wake up!" I shouted.

"Huh?" Zeus jumped up. "Where are my T-bolts? Somebody get my bucket!"

"Easy, Dad," said Athena. "It's only Hades."

"What are *you* doing up here, Hades?" Hera asked. "It's never good news when you show up."

I ignored the insult and began to make my case. "This war," I said, "has gone on for nine years!"

"Let's go for nine more!" cried Ares.

I shot him a look. "My kingdom is so crowded that my ghosts are doubled up in bunk beds!"

"So?" said Aphrodite. "What's the *problema*?"

"You immortals," I went on, "have been quick to help your favorites fight on the plain of Troy. Now be as quick to help them *end* the war!"

"Why should we?" asked Po, who happened to be up on Mount Olympus that day. From the looks of him, I guessed he'd come to visit the Immortals' Beauty Salon for a long-overdue touch-up of his blue hair.

"I'll tell you why," I said. "Because fewer mortals on earth means fewer sacrifices for the gods."

"He's got a point," said Hephaestus, god of the forge. "We haven't been getting many smoky sacrifices since this war started."

"I'm all for ending the war," Apollo said, "as long as the Trojans win."

"No, the Greeks must win," declared Athena.

"That's right," said Hera. "The Greeks!"

My godly heart sank. Why had I even bothered coming up here? The gods were hopeless!

Just then, a door banged open, and silver-footed Thetis raced in.

"Thetis!" thundered Zeus. "What's wrong? You look terrible."

"I need help!" cried Thetis. "Achilles is mad with grief over the death of Patroclus."

"It's always something with that boy of hers," Hera muttered. She was well aware of Zeus's little flirtation with Thetis.

The sea goddess spotted Hephaestus in the

crowd and ran over to him. "My son's armor has been taken by Hector!" she cried. "Achilles must have new armor!"

Hephaestus nodded. "I can make him armor," he said. "Come back in six weeks."

"He needs it by dawn tomorrow!" Thetis cried.

"A rush job," said Hephaestus. "That'll cost you."

"I'll pay for it, Hephaestus," I offered. I am the god of wealth, after all. It was the least I could do.

"Come to my forge, Thetis," Hephaestus said. "You, too, Hades. You shall see me make Achilles a suit of armor like no other!"

Hephaestus's forge was a vast space filled with fiery furnaces and smoke. It reminded me of Tartarus, the punishment fields down in my kingdom.

Hephaestus picked up his bellows, made from the hides of twenty oxen, and pumped them until his fires raged. Then with a great huge hammer, he began pounding sheets of bronze, silver, and gold together to make a shield.

Hephaestus's hammer banged and banged, but I was so used to noise from the war that I dozed off. When I opened my eyes, I was nearly blinded by the glow of newly made armor.

"Behold, Thetis!" Hephaestus cried, proudly holding up his creations. "I have made for your son a breastplate, a golden helmet, guards for his shins, and a wondrous shield."

I stared at that shield. The inlaid brass, silver, and gold formed images of lions and panthers, corn and grapes, cities and seas.

"This is armor like no other," Thetis said. "Strong and glowing! But I wonder — could you make him two more pieces?"

"You want *more*?" cried Hephaestus.

"Heel protectors," said Thetis. "Small items, really."

Hephaestus turned back to his forge. He quickly pounded out two cup-shaped armored pieces with brass chains to fasten them to the shin guards.

"Thank you, Hephaestus!" Thetis said. "Dawn will soon break — I must go. I am in your debt."

"A nice lobster dinner one of these nights?" Hephaestus called after her, but silver-footed Thetis was already far away.

ZZZZZZIP!

I caught up with her in the Greek camp just before sun up. She was looking for Achilles.

"Oh, Hades," Thetis said as we walked together through the camp. "It seems like only yesterday that I dipped Achilles into the River Styx."

I nodded. "Time passes so quickly."

". . . for mortals," Thetis added, catching sight of her son. "Achilles!" she called, breaking into a run. "Achilles!"

I watched her go as the sun peeked over the horizon. It would be daylight soon. Time for me to go undercover — *POOF!*

Minutes later, Achilles appeared. He walked out of his camp decked out in his gleaming new armor. But — was he limping?

Thetis ran after him. "May the gods protect you, Achilles!" she called.

Achilles stopped, bent down, and fiddled with

his armor. When he stood up again, he held out the heel protectors.

"They give me blisters, Mom," he said.

"A small price to pay!" cried Thetis.

But Achilles dropped the heel protectors into her hands and began to climb up the Greek wall. When he reached the top, the sunlight hit his armor, and he shone so brightly that all who saw him gasped.

"I am coming for you, Hector!" Achilles roared.

"Not so fast," said Odysseus, stepping up beside him. "First, you must make peace with Agamemnon."

Achilles clenched his fists. "Okay, okay," he said.

The two walked to the High King's camp. I walked invisibly behind them.

"Agamemnon!" said Achilles when they found him. "Sorry we fought."

"Me, too," said Agamemnon.

"I blame Eris, goddess of discord," said Achilles.

"Me, too," said Agamemnon. "Now, let's go get those Trojans!"

"Hold it!" cried Odysseus. "Don't you two know anything? You have to make a sacrifice to the gods first."

They gathered all the Greek warriors around and sent up a nice smoky offering.

"*Now* can we fight?" asked Achilles.

"Can we?" asked Agamemnon.

"Let's do it!" cried Odysseus. "And let's win this thing. If I don't get home soon, Penelope's going to kill me."

With ear-splitting battle cries, the Greeks rushed out at the Trojans, slashing them with swords, bashing them with rocks. Achilles sprang into his chariot and galloped into battle. When they saw him in his gleaming armor, the Trojans, heroes and all, turned tail and ran for the safety of their city.

I headed for the city and saw King Priam sitting on the wall, watching the battle. Not far from him sat Helen.

ZZZZZZIP!

"Helen?" I whispered.

"Is that you, Hades?" she whispered back.

"It's me," I said. "I'm sitting next to you."

Helen nodded. She wore a woven gown of blue and red. The same red as Menelaus's hair. *Could the Smoochie Woochie be weakening?* I wondered.

Together we watched the Trojans running away from the Greek army. As they neared the city, King Priam cried, "Open the gates! Let our warriors in!"

Priam's men began opening the great gates.

"When our soldiers are in, close the gates!" ordered the king. "Take care not to let a single Greek get in!"

The Trojan warriors raced for the city.

"Run!" Helen called to them. "Run!"

"Are you for Troy now?" I whispered.

"I am for no more killing," she said.

"Me, too," I told her. "Me, too."

At last only a single Trojan soldier remained on the field. The Greek army was closing in on him.

"Come in!" King Priam shouted down to him. "We must shut the gates!"

The warrior turned to face the city. It was mighty Hector.

"Hector!" cried his father. "You must hurry!"

"I shall stay here!" Hector called back.

"No, my son!" cried Priam. "Come inside! I beg you!"

Hector shook his head as the Greeks galloped toward him. King Priam's men began to shut the gates.

"Run, Hector!" the king cried desperately. "There is no shame in saving yourself."

But Hector stayed where he was.

As the Greeks closed in on Hector, Agamemnon cried, "Halt!"

The soldiers reined in their horses, and Achilles jumped from his chariot. With a great angry roar, he ran at Hector.

I waited for Hector to draw his sword. Or throw his spear. Or charge at Achilles. But he stood where he was. And then suddenly — he took off running.

Achilles looked stunned. And then he raced off after him.

Hector stuck close to the wall as he ran. Achilles chased him, and they both vanished behind the city.

What was Hector thinking? Did he have a plan? Or had he lost his mind?

"Here they come!" yelled a Trojan from atop the wall as the runners reappeared, circling around to the front.

Hector sped past the gates of Troy and kept on running. Twice he circled the city with Achilles right behind him. They circled the city a third time. And then Hector stopped. He turned to face Achilles.

Was this some crazy scheme to confuse the Greek hero? If so, it wasn't working.

Achilles hurled a spear at Hector. It sailed past his ear, just missing him.

Now Hector heaved a spear. It hit Achilles's magnificent shield and bounced off. Hector drew his sword and ran at Achilles.

Achilles had one spear left, and he sent it

flying. It struck Hector's neck, and the great Trojan warrior went down.

The great Greek warrior stood over the dying Trojan. "Now I have avenged the death of Patroclus!" Achilles cried.

"My fate . . . is to die now," Hector said haltingly. "Your fate . . . will come soon."

"I am fated to die in battle," admitted Achilles. "But my time has not yet come."

Hector struggled to breathe as he said, "At these very gates . . . Paris shall take your life."

"*Paris?*" said Achilles. "I don't think so."

Hector spoke no more.

Feeling low, I turned away, knowing that when I got back to the Underworld, Hector, the greatest Trojan hero, would be among my ghosts.

CHAPTER XII

MEANWHILE, IN THE UNDERWORLD

Hector wasn't in my kingdom when I arrived. But a few weeks later, when I went down to the Styx, Charon was ferrying him across the river.

Hector stepped ashore and gave his name to Hypnos, who was trying to keep track of the ghosts. With the constant stream of newcomers, it was a huge task.

"Hector," I said as he walked toward me, "what took you so long to get here?"

He shrugged. "Some problem with my burial."

I nodded. That happened sometimes. Mortals must wander outside my kingdom until they are properly buried.

"Just follow the others to Motel Styx," I told him, pointing.

"Motel?" Hector said. "What is a 'motel'?"

"An inn," I said. "Don't worry, you won't be there long. You'll be judged and most likely sent to the peaceful apple orchards of Elysium."

"What?" cried Hector.

"That's the eternal reward for mortals who have been good in life," I told him.

"I am a warrior!" cried Hector. "I like fighting and slaying my enemies! Can I do this in Elysium?"

"Not really," I told him. "But in time, you'll get used to peace."

Hector groaned and looked back at Charon's River Taxi as if he were thinking of making a break for it. Charon was unloading a new batch of ghosts. "Who's *that*?" Hector suddenly asked.

I turned and saw the ghost of a tall young woman walking off the River Taxi. She was almost as beautiful as Helen.

"Let's go find out," I said, and I walked with Hector back to the riverbank.

"Name?" Hypnos asked the young woman as she stepped ashore.

"Penthesilea," she replied.

"P-E-N . . ." muttered Hypnos, trying to write it down. "Aw, never mind. Occupation?"

"What?" said Penthesilea.

"I'll take it from here, Hypnos," I said, stepping forward. He needed help keeping track of the ghosts. Maybe when Persephone came home, she'd be willing to pitch in.

"Welcome to the Underworld, Penthesilea," I said. "Come on, Hector. I'll walk you both over to Motel Styx."

"You look too young to have died of old age," Hector said as we started off.

I smiled to myself. Not a bad Underworld pick-up line.

"I was slain in battle at Troy," said Penthesilea.

"Me, too!" Hector exclaimed. "But . . . I never saw you on the battlefield. If I had, I'd definitely remember."

"I was Queen of the Amazons," Penthesilea

told him. "We are a nation of brave women warriors."

"I've heard of you," Hector said. "I'm Hector, by the way."

"I've heard of you," said Penthesilea. "I arrived in Troy shortly after you were killed. I led my warriors onto the battlefield. We have no chariots, but ride on the backs of fiery white steeds. All the Trojans cheered us on."

"I'll bet," said Hector.

"With a great war cry, I galloped toward the Greek army," Penthesilea went on. "My warriors galloped after me. The Greeks thought they need not fear us, but we took down many of their warriors."

"And then?" said Hector.

"And then a Greek soldier threw his javelin and knocked me from my steed," said Penthesilea. "My helmet fell off, and as I lay dying, the Greek soldier looked at my face and seemed to fall in love with me. 'I am Achilles' he said. 'Please forgive me!' But it was too late for that."

"Achilles killed me, too!" cried Hector. He seemed thrilled to have something in common with the Amazon queen. "But my brother Paris shall slay him," he added.

"Paris?" said Penthesilea. "The one in that crazy panther outfit?"

Hector nodded. "Achilles will join us here soon," he said. "You'll see."

I stopped and let Hector and Penthesilea continue on to Motel Styx without me. They didn't seem to notice.

* * *

When fall arrived, Persephone came home to the Underworld. Was I ever happy to see her! I was hoping she could take my mind off the endless war in Troy.

One night, Thanatos built us a roaring fire in the fireplace. Cerbie lay in front of it, warming his heads, while P-phone and I talked and played a little Scrabble.

"Any new Trojan rescuers arrive lately,

Hades?" Persephone asked, playing the word *DAISY*.

"There's always some new hero showing up to save Troy," I said.

I used the *S* in *DAISY* to play *SWORD*.

"Nice one, Hades," Persephone said, studying the board.

"Memnon is the most recent hero," I went on. "He and his men came from Ethiopia and traveled for years to get to Troy."

Persephone used the *R* in *SWORD* to make ROSE.

"The Trojans set their hopes on Memnon," I added, playing the word *STAB*. "But Achilles slew him."

"Poor Memnon," said Persepone, spelling out *PETUNIAS* on the board, and scoring bonus points for using all seven of her letters.

"Your words are all flowers," I pointed out. "Is that fair?"

"Of course it is, Hades," she said. "And look, yours are all war words. You can't stop thinking about that war, can you?"

I shook my head. "It really gets to me," I told her.

"Why don't I come with you tomorrow to meet the River Taxi?" Persephone suggested. "I'll keep you company."

"I'd love that, P-phone," I said.

* * *

True to her word, Persephone rode with me to the bank of the River Styx. Cerbie wasn't too happy about not sitting shotgun, but he and Persephone were friends these days, so he didn't growl or make a fuss about sitting in the back.

When we arrived at the river, Charon's ferryboat was just pulling in. We hopped out of the chariot.

"Some of these ghosts are pretty roughed up," I warned Persephone.

"I understand," she said. "Who's that? He looks like some kind of hero."

I followed her gaze and my godly knees nearly buckled out from under me.

"Achilles!" I cried.

At the sound of his name, the great Greek hero looked around. When he saw me, he cut out of line and headed over.

"Excuse me?" said Hypnos as he passed by. "Excuse me! I need your name!"

"It's Achilles, Hypnos," I said as the hero approached. "With two L's."

"King Hades, Queen Persephone," Achilles said, bowing. Clearly, Thetis had raised him to respect the gods.

"I hoped you wouldn't come down to my kingdom so soon, Achilles," I said.

"Hector was right!" cried Achilles, his eyes flashing. "Paris slew me!"

"Let's go and sit beside the Pool of Memory while you tell your tale, Achilles," said Persephone. His ghost and I followed her over to the pool. The three of us sat down on benches beneath the poplar trees. "Now tell us what happened," she said.

"I had just slain Memnon," Achilles said. "I was running among the Trojans, slashing and taking them down. Many soldiers ran for the city. King Priam ordered the gates of Troy to be flung open, and a huge rush of men tried to get into the city. I, too, ran for the gates. I stood between them, slaying those who ran for safety. I caught sight of Paris standing on the palace steps, far from the fighting."

"As usual," I muttered.

"Paris fit an arrow into his bow," Achilles went on. "And I saw a white glow surround him."

"Sounds like Apollo," I said. "He glows with a white light when he appears to mortals."

"Paris shot his arrow high into the air, missing the Trojans who stood between us," said Achilles. "The arrow landed in the dust at my feet just as a Trojan warrior lunged at me with his sword. I jumped back to avoid being stabbed and stepped on the arrow. It pierced my heel."

"The one your mother held you by when she dipped you into the Styx?" I asked.

Achilles nodded. "My only vulnerable spot. Had it been an ordinary arrow, it would have made a small wound," he added. "But the instant it pierced my skin, I felt a terrible sickness coarse through my blood. As I dropped to the ground, I knew that Paris had shot me with a poisoned arrow."

My ichor was steaming! Paris was a coward. And Apollo would stop at nothing to help the Trojans win the war. Yet Achilles had been fated to die in battle, and so he did.

The great warrior stared into the Pool of Memory and said no more.

Persephone and I rose and walked quietly away, leaving him to his memories. Soon Achilles would be sent to Elysium where he would live in eternal peace, no easy task for a great warrior.

When we reached my chariot, Cerbie hopped into the backseat.

"Good dog!" I said, slipping him three of the little Ambro-Bacon Bits I always carry in my pocket.

As she climbed into the front seat, Persephone said, "Now I understand why you think of nothing but this war, Hades."

I sat down in the driver's seat and picked up the reins. "Will it never end?"

"Go up to Troy, Hades," Persephone said. "Talk to Odysseus."

"But there's so much work to do down here," I told her. "I can't leave."

"Yes, you can, Hades," she said. "I'll keep things going down here, and the Furies will help me."

"I don't know. . . ." I began.

"Go, Hades," said Persephone. "Maybe clever Odysseus can come up with a way to end the war."

CHAPTER XIII

THE BOW OF HERCULES

I decided Persephone was right. She almost always is.

ZZZZZZIP!

I landed invisibly inside Troy. I was about to *ZIP!* over to the Greek camp when I heard King Priam say, "Let's give a hero's welcome to the grandson of Hercules!"

The grandson of Hercules? This I had to see.

I walked around a corner to find clapping, cheering Trojans gathered around a tall, muscle-bound young man. Standing against a wall away from the crowd was Helen. I hurried over.

"Helen?" I whispered. "It's me, Hades."

"I'm glad you're here," Helen said softly. "What do you think of the latest hero to ride to the rescue of Troy?"

"He looks about as big and strong as his grandpa," I said.

"I shall slay countless Greeks!" Hercules's grandson boasted. "I shall send them running for their ships!"

"That's the spirit!" King Priam cried. "With the grandson of Hercules on our side, Troy will win this war!"

I leaned toward Helen. "I'm going to the Greek camp to see what's going on," I whispered. "Good to see you, Helen."

"Don't go!" Helen begged. "Come sit on the wall with me where we can talk."

I walked behind her as she started up the stairs to the top of the wall. Halfway up, she missed a step and lost her balance. I caught her before she fell and *POOF!* Helen vanished.

"Hades?" she said. "What just happened?"

"It's the Helmet," I said. "It makes me and

whatever I'm holding disappear. I'll keep hold of you until we get up the stairs, and then I'll let go."

"No, wait!" said Helen. "I've been a prisoner behind these walls for nine years! Take me with you to the Greek camp. Please?"

It hit me then that Helen hadn't seen Menelaus in all that time. Maybe if she saw him, it would finally put an end to the Smoochie Woochie's power. Maybe she'd fall in love with him all over again. Maybe the war would end, and he'd take her back to Sparta.

"Hang on tight!" I said.

ZZZZZZZZZZZZZZZZZZIP!

We touched down outside Agamemnon's tent. Loud voices sounded from inside. The Greek leaders seemed to be having a meeting.

I inched us closer to a gap in the tent where we could peer in.

Menelaus stood at the center of the tent. "Odysseus, you have the god-forged armor of Achilles!" he was saying. "Will you fight the grandson of Hercules?"

This was it — Helen's first glimpse of Menelaus in nine years!

"His hair," she whispered. "It isn't red any more."

I sighed. Helen was Helen. What did I expect?

"I can't defeat the grandson of Hercules," Odysseus said. "But I know who can."

"Who? Who?" cried the other Greeks.

"The son of Achilles," Odysseus replied.

"Achilles had no son!" cried Agamemnon.

"Ah, but he did," said Odysseus. "Achilles was secretly married to a princess of Scyros. She bore him a son, Pyrrhus. He was a boy when Achilles left for war, but Pyrrhus must be a man by now."

"A vision! I'm having a vision!" cried the prophet Calchas, leaping to his feet. "It has been revealed to me that the Greeks cannot take Troy unless a son of Achilles comes to slay the grandson of Hercules!"

"That's not a vision," said Agamemnon. "We were just talking about that."

"That's my vision," said Calchas. "Take it or leave it."

"My men will row me to Scyros," Odysseus went on, "and we shall return with Pyrrhus."

"Yes!" cried Menelaus. "Tell Pyrrhus that if he comes to fight for the Greeks, I shall give him the hand of my daughter Hermione in marriage."

"Of all the nerve!" whispered Helen.

Between Menelaus's graying hair and his willingness to give his daughter to a complete stranger, my plan for Helen to fall in love with him again wasn't working out too well.

"I'll take you back to Troy now, Helen," I whispered.

ZZZZZZZZZZZZZZIP!

* * *

The following week, I astro-traveled to Scyros, where Pyrrhus lived. It wasn't long before Odysseus showed up.

"Wait here," he told his oarsmen. "I'll be back."

He took a package from the ship and started up the road to Scyros.

I caught up with him and pulled off my Helmet — *FOOP!*

"Hades!" Odysseus exclaimed when I appeared at his side. "What brings you to Scyros?"

"You do, Odysseus," I said as we walked along. "Tell me the truth. Do you really think the son of Achilles can end this war?"

"That's what the prophet Calchus said," Odysseus answered.

"But what do *you* think?" I said.

Before Odysseus could answer, a javelin came flying through the air. Right behind it ran a giant of a young man. He reached out and grabbed the shaft of the javelin just after the tip hit the ground.

"Almost!" cried the young man. As he bent down to pick up the javelin, he noticed us.

"I once knew a man who could throw a javelin and catch it before it hit the ground," Odysseus called. "His name was Achilles."

"Achilles is my father!" cried the young man, and he ran over to us.

"I know," said Odysseus. "You look just like him." He thrust the package into the young man's hands.

Pyrrhus opened the package. "Armor!" he cried.

"It's not just any armor," I told him. "This armor was made for your father by Hephaestus, god of the forge."

"Cool!" said Pyrrhus. He put the armor on. It fit him perfectly. "I love it! But I don't really need armor living here in peaceful Scyros."

"That's what we've come to talk to you about," said Odysseus.

After hearing what Odysseus had to say, Pyrrhus ran off to tell his grandfather the king and his mother the princess that he was going to Troy to slay the grandson of Hercules.

"Don't go!" begged his mother. "Look what happened to your father."

"I'll be careful," said Pyrrhus, and off he went with Odysseus to the ship.

"See you in Troy!" I called as they rowed out to sea.

* * *

Before I went back to Troy, I made a quick trip
to the Underworld to see how Persephone and
the Furies were handling the daily flood of new
ghosts.

I was impressed! Persephone had talked the
Underworld carpenters into adding two new
wings to Motel Styx. And with the Furies glaring
at the ghosts with their glowing red eyes and
rattling their scourges, there was very little
howling or moaning.

By the time I got back up to Troy, Pyrrhus had
already slain Hercules's grandson.

But did that stop the war?

It did not.

Every morning, the Greeks picked up their
weapons and stormed the city. And every
evening, they returned to their camp with the
walls of Troy still standing.

One night, I put on my Helmet — *POOF!* —
and traveled to the Greek camp, hoping to hear
talk of a plan to end the war.

"Maybe we'll take Troy tomorrow," Agamemnon said.

That wasn't much of a plan.

"Calchas?" said Odysseus. "Have you had any visions lately that might help us win this war and sail home to Greece?"

"I am having a vision as we speak!" Calchas cried. "It is revealed to me that Troy cannot be taken without the Bow of Hercules!"

"The Bow of Hercules?" cried Odysseus. "But that belonged to Philoctetes! He had that smelly wound. And he wouldn't stop howling. So we . . . sort of . . . left him all alone on that island . . . to die."

"Go to the island!" cried Calchas. "Ask Philoctetes to give you the Bow!"

Odysseus gasped. "He's alive?"

Calchas nodded.

"But he must know we deserted him!" cried Odysseus. "He's not going to say, 'Okay, here's the Bow of Hercules.' He's going to shoot at us with the Poisoned Arrows of Hercules!"

"Tell Philoctetes to come to Troy with you,

bringing the Bow of Hercules," Calchas said. "Tell him that in Troy, his wound shall be healed."

"Oh, brother," muttered Odysseus. "Pyrrhus, you come with me. Philoctetes never saw you, so he has no reason not to trust you."

The next morning the two sailed for the deserted island. I intended to go back to the Underworld, but I thought Odysseus might need a little godly help dealing with Philoctetes. Those poison-tipped Arrows of his were no joke.

When I figured they were almost there, I *ZZZZZZIPPED!* to their ship.

"The boat's rocking!" said Pyrrhus when I landed invisibly on the deck.

"Boats rock," said Odysseus. "Now, are you clear on our plan?"

Pyrrhus nodded. "I go to the cave of Philo . . . Philo . . ."

"Philoctetes," Odysseus said.

"Right," said Pyrrhus. "I tell him I left Troy because you and I quarreled. I tell him I've come to rescue him."

"And then what?" asked Odysseus.

"And then I offer to carry the Bow and Arrows and help him down to the ship," Pyrrhus went on. "And when he gives me the Bow and Arrows, I run to the ship and we sail away."

"Exactly!" Odysseus said.

Pyrrhus frowned. "I'm not very good at lying," he said.

"It's the only way," said Odysseus, who was a born liar.

When we reached the island, we went ashore. Near the cave, Odysseus hid in the bushes. I stuck invisibly with Pyrrhus as he walked closer.

"Pew!" Pyrrhus muttered. He stopped and shouted, "Philo . . . Philo . . . Hey, Phil?"

Philoctetes limped to the cave entrance. "Who calls me?" he cried.

"I am Pyrrhus! Son of Achilles!" shouted Pyrrhus. "I was in Troy, but I quarreled! I will carry your Bow and Arrows!"

"Huh?" said Philoctetes.

"To the ship!" Pyrrhus exclaimed. "We sail away!"

"You're not making any sense," Philoctetes

said. "But I need rescuing, so here, take my Bow and Arrows."

Pyrrhus held his breath, walked over to the smelly Philoctetes, and took his Bow and Arrows. But when he saw how eager the poor man was to be rescued, he couldn't bring himself to run away and leave him.

"No, you carry them," Pyrrhus said, trying to hand the Bow and Arrows back.

Hearing this, Odysseus leaped out of the bushes, shouting, "Give me the Bow of Hercules!"

"Odysseus!" cried Philoctetes, stumbling back in surprise. "You left me here to die." He turned back to Pyrrhus. "Give me the Bow and Arrows of Hercules!"

"Uh . . ." said Pyrrhus.

"Give them here!" ordered Odysseus.

"Um . . ." said Pyrrhus.

Readers, you know I don't like to interfere in the lives of mortals, but I didn't want anyone getting shot with a poisoned arrow. This was a time for some godly intervention.

ZZZZZZIP!

I landed on Mount Olympus outside Hercules's palace. I ran inside and ripped off my Helmet — *FOOP!*

"Hercules, come with me, quick!" I told him. "You have to tell Philoctetes to forgive Odysseus and go to Troy."

"Hey, Hades!" said Hercules. "How is my old buddy, Philoctetes?"

"Not good," I told him. "No time to explain. Let's go." I jammed my Helmet back on. *POOF!*

ZZZZZZZZZZZIP!

Hercules appeared suddenly in front of the three mortals. I just hoped Pyrrhus would have enough sense not to say anything about slaying his grandson.

"Hercules!" cried the astonished Philoctetes.

"Whoa," said Hercules, stepping back from his poor, smelly friend. "Listen, you have to forgive Odysseus."

"No way!" said Philoctetes.

"Yes, way," said Hercules. "And you have to go with him to Troy."

"But why?" asked Philoctetes.

"Uh, I'm a little cloudy on that," Hercules said. "But we're friends, right? Trust me on this, buddy."

"If you say so." Philoctetes turned to Odysseus and said, "I forgive you."

"Let's hit the road!" said Odysseus.

I waited for Odysseus to apologize for stranding the poor wounded man on a deserted island for ten years, but apparently that wasn't his way.

"Now I really will help you to the ship, Phil," Pyrrhus said. Ignoring the stench, he took Philoctetes's arm, and they started down the hill. "The prophet Calchas says your wound will be healed when we reach Troy."

"No kidding," said Philoctetes.

"Oh, boy," muttered Odysseus as he set off after them. "It's gonna be a long, stinky voyage back to Troy."

As the mortals boarded their ship to sail back to Troy, I took off my Helmet. *FOOP!*

Hercules turned to me. "What was that about?" he asked.

"Let's go back up to Mount Olympus, Herc," I said. "I'll buy you a necta-brewsky at the Gods and Monsters Pub and tell you all about it."

ZZZZZZZZZZZZZZZIP!

CHAPTER XIV

THE TROJAN HORSE

A few weeks later, I returned to Troy. The war was still raging, but now the Trojans had a new tactic. Warriors no longer ran out of the city each day to fight. Instead, the gates of Troy stayed closed, and archers stood on top of the wall, shooting arrows down at the Greeks.

The Greek archers couldn't shoot arrows high enough to take out the Trojan archers, so as long as those gates stayed shut, there was no way the Greeks could take Troy.

Unseen, I *ZZZZZZIPPED!* over to the Greek camp to find out what was going on. I stopped by Philoctetes's tent. His wound was on the mend and hardly stunk at all.

While I was there, Agamemnon came by. "How's it going, Philoctetes?" he asked the famous archer.

"Feelin' good," Philoctetes said. "Ready to let some Arrows of Hercules fly." He rattled the Arrows in his quiver. "Know what's on these babies?"

Agamemnon shook his head.

"Hydra blood," Philoctetes said. "The strongest poison ever."

"We Greeks never shoot poisoned arrows!" declared Agamemnon.

"How long have you been here in Troy?" Philoctetes asked.

"Ten years," said Agamemnon.

"Let's try it my way," said Philoctetes, and this time, Agamemnon didn't object.

The next day, when the Greek warriors rushed toward Troy, Philoctetes was with them. As usual, Trojan archers stood atop the Trojan wall, shooting arrows at the Greeks as they came.

Philoctetes's eyes searched among the Trojan archers standing on the wall. When he saw Paris, he notched an Arrow into the Bow of Hercules and shouted, "Hey there, handsome!"

Paris looked down. "Who's calling me?"

"Your fate!" Philoctetes cried, and he sent the Arrow flying.

Paris saw it coming and turned away. The Arrow barely nicked his hand, but that was enough. Paris fell backwards from the wall.

ZZZZZZIP!

Inside the city walls, all was chaos. I hurried to Helen's weaving room. She sat at her loom, looking stunned.

FOOP!

"Helen?" I said.

She looked up at me with tears in her eyes. "Paris has been slain," she said softly. "I feel it somehow."

"Helen?" someone shouted.

I hardly had time to put my Helmet back on — *POOF!* — before Deiphobus, one of Paris's brothers, came in.

"I see you've heard the news, Helen," he said. "You cannot go back to Menelaus now. All the Greeks are against you. You will be safe at my house. Come!"

Helen rose and followed him from the room.

I wondered, would Deiphobus protect her? And was it true that the Greeks had turned against her? As soon as possible, I went to see Helen again. She sat in Deiphobus's house, weaving.

Nothing had changed! Nothing! Helen kept weaving, and the Greeks and Trojans kept fighting.

I was sick of it all!

After dark, I *ZZZZZIPPED!* invisibly down to the Greek camp, where Agamemnon, Menelaus, Philoctetes, Odysseus, and the other leaders sat in a circle with Calchas.

"Calchas," Agamemnon was saying, "you claimed that if we brought Philoctetes and the Bow of Hercules to Troy, we'd take the city."

"I didn't say that would do it for sure," said Calchas. "What I *said* was that you couldn't win the war *without* Philoctetes and the Bow of Hercules."

"Seers can be so annoying," Odysseys said, running a finger along the blade of his sword. "So what do we need to do to take Troy, Cal?"

Calchas closed his eyes. "I see a vision!" he murmured. "A vision of the Palladium!"

"You mean that little statue of Athena?" asked Menelaus. "The one that fell from Mount Olympus?"

"That's the one." Calchas nodded. "As long as the Palladium stands in the city, the Greeks cannot take Troy."

"I'll go get it, then," Odysseus said. He rose to his feet and picked up his pack.

I hurried invisibly after Odysseus to see what he was up to. He was a clever mortal, but I doubted that even *he* could find a way to get inside the high walls surrounding Troy.

I followed him to the foothills of Mount Ida, behind Troy. Odysseus walked until he came to a stream. There, he picked up a big stone and began beating himself in the head with it until he was battered and bleeding. Next, he took a cloak from his pack. He ripped it and beat it with rocks until it was no more than a rag.

Had it been any other mortal, I'd have thought he'd lost his mind. But with Odysseus, I figured he was working on some sort of scheme.

At dawn, the bruised and swollen-faced Odysseus put on his ragged cloak and walked to the gates of Troy. When the Trojan cattlemen drove their cattle out through the gates, he made his way into the city, crying, "Scraps! Give a poor beggar some scraps!"

In those days, people were kind to beggars who were down on their luck and often let them sleep in temples.

I kept an eye on Odysseus as he spent the day inside Troy begging for food. Toward evening, he made his way to Deiphobus's house, and there, beside a fountain, Helen sat knitting.

"Any scraps for a poor beggar?" Odysseus asked, holding out a dirty hand.

Helen looked up at him and frowned. "Don't I know you?" she said.

"Once I was your suitor," the beggar said. "But I married your cousin instead."

Helen's eyes widened. "Odysseus!" she whispered. "You are in great danger here!"

"I've come to ask you an important question," Odysseus said, keeping his voice low. "Do you still love Menelaus?"

Helen looked around, afraid someone might overhear. "I do," she said softly. "Aphrodite had Cupid shoot me with an arrow, and I fell in love with Paris. But when he died, the spell was broken."

"I will tell Menelaus," said Odysseus. "Who knows? Maybe one day you shall sail with him back to Sparta."

"I hope so," said Helen.

"One more thing," Odysseus said. He kept his voice low as he told Helen his plan to take the Paladium, but with my godly hearing, I didn't miss a word.

* * *

When the cattlemen left Troy the next morning, Odysseus left along with them. But on a dark night, when the moon was no more than a sliver, he snuck back into the city. Helen had arranged for the priests guarding the Palladium to be away from their posts that night, so he had no trouble stealing the little statue. By means of a rope, he went back over the wall, making a quick exit from Troy.

At daybreak, Odysseus found Calchas.

"Here is the Palladium," said Odysseus, showing him the statue. "Now can we take Troy?"

"Absolutely!" said Calchas.

For days, the Greeks battered the gates of Troy. The Trojans ran out of arrows, so they began throwing rocks down at the Greeks.

Disgusted with the constant war, I went back to my kingdom. When I returned to Troy weeks later, I found the Greeks exhausted from fighting and the Trojans still safe within their city walls.

Wearing my Helmet, I went once more to the Greek camp.

"I have a vision!" Calchas was saying as the fires burned low.

"Whatever it is," said Odysseus, "I have a better idea."

All the Greeks turned toward Odysseus to hear what he had to say.

"In secret, we shall build a wooden horse," Odysseus began. "A horse big enough so that twelve armed men can hide inside its belly."

"That's crazy," said Calchas.

"We shall place the horse with soldiers inside on the plain outside of Troy," Odysseus went on.

"Terrible idea!" cried Calchas.

"Then all the Greek ships will sail away as if they're heading home," Odysseus continued. "But really they'll only sail around the bend and wait there, out of sight. One brave man not known to the Trojans shall stay behind."

"What's the point?" said Calchas.

"You'll see," said Odysseus.

* * *

Over the next weeks, as I came and went, I saw Greeks sneak into the forests of Mount Ida to cut down trees. I saw the giant horse from Odysseus's plan begin to take shape.

And then one night I arrived, wearing my Helmet of Darkness, and there was the wooden horse standing on the plain outside the gates of Troy. The Greeks had set fire to their camp and were sailing off.

The plan was underway!

At dawn, the Trojan cattlemen drove their herds out of the city. They saw the giant horse. They saw the Greek camp burning and the ships sailing away.

"They're gone!" cried one of the cattlemen, running back into the city. "The Greeks are going back to Greece!"

Trojan soldiers ran to the smoldering Greek camp to investigate. They found the camp deserted and raced back to the city, shouting the news.

The gates of Troy were thrown open. Old men, women, girls, and boys who had been walled up inside their city for ten long years poured out onto the plain.

Priam's sons and daughters helped the old king out onto the plain. Helen stood beside him as they gazed in wonder at the horse.

Helen glanced over to where the Greek ships had been anchored. She seemed sad to have been left behind in Troy.

How I wished I could speak to her! But now was not the time.

A man dressed in priestly robes came out of Troy. When he saw the giant horse, he began shouting, "Don't touch it! Leave it be! It's some trick of the Greeks!"

"Oh, take it easy, Laocoon!" said a Trojan man. "It's just a wooden horse."

"It's big enough to have men hidden inside!" cried Laocoon. He grabbed a spear from a nearby soldier and heaved it at the horse.

THONK! The spear bounced off.

"Hear that?" the priest cried. "The horse is hollow!"

But before Laocoon could say another

word, Trojan soldiers hurried up to King Priam dragging a Greek prisoner.

"We found him hiding near the ruins of the camp," a soldier told the king. "He says his name is Sinon."

"My people tried to kill me!" Sinon cried.

"Why should we believe you?" asked a Trojan soldier.

"A seer told the Greeks that if they wanted a safe trip home, they must sacrifice one of their men!" wailed Sinon. "I was chosen! My comrades tied me up. They planned to kill me when the great horse was finished, but I escaped and hid until they sailed off."

"What do you know about this horse?" asked King Priam.

"Athena was angry at the Greeks for stealing the Palladium," said Sinon. "We built the horse as a peace offering to the goddess. A seer told us that if the Trojans destroy the horse, Athena will destroy their city."

"Sinon has suffered enough at the hands of his own people," declared the king. "Untie him!"

"Thank you, thank you!" cried Sinon.

"If this is a peace offering for Athena," said the king, "then we must bring it into the city."

"No!" Laocoon shouted. "It's a trick, I tell you! A trick!"

The words were hardly out of his mouth when a pair of giant serpents reared up out of the sea. Their scaled bodies glistened as they moved swiftly across the plain toward Laocoon. They grabbed him up in their coils, squeezed the life out of him, and dropped him at the feet of the great horse. Then, as quickly as they'd come, they vanished back into the sea.

"The priest stuck the horse with a spear!" cried a Trojan man.

"Athena sent the serpents to punish him!" cried another.

More likely my bro Po had sent them. He was for the Greeks, after all.

"Bring ropes!" ordered King Priam. "And make a wheeled cart! Hurry! We shall take the horse to the temple where the Palladium once stood."

The Trojans were falling for the Greeks' plan hook, line, and sinker.

Cassandra came out of the city now and ran to the king. "Do not bring this horse into the city, father!" she cried. "If you do, Troy will go up in flames!"

"Zip it, Cassandra," one of her brothers said. "The horse is going in."

It didn't take long for the Trojans to build a wheeled platform and roll the horse into their city. They put it in the square outside Athena's temple, and everyone danced around it, singing and celebrating the end of the long war.

"The war is over!" cried a soldier, raising a cup of wine.

"We have a big horse!" cried another, lifting his cup.

"A peace offering!" cried still another. "What could be bad?"

Long after midnight, the Trojans staggered off to their homes and fell into a happy sleep.

I kept a godly eye on Sinon. He waited until all was quiet, then he climbed to the top of the wall and lit a torch. He waved it, signaling the Greek ships to return.

Next Sinon hurried to the great wooden horse. He hooted like a night owl to let the men inside know that the time had come for taking Troy.

I heard the snap of wooden bolts. The trap door in the belly of the horse opened. One by one, silent as shadows, Odysseus, Menelaus, and the rest of the heroes slid down a rope.

Sinon returned to the top of the wall. Invisibly, I joined him there and saw that the Greek ships had returned. Warriors streamed out of those ships. They were charging silently up the Trojan plain.

Sinon and the Greek warriors who'd been hidden inside the horse ran to the gates of Troy. They slew the guards and opened the gates. The Greek army raced into the city, lighting fires as they came.

All was confusion as the Trojans woke to find their city aflame and filled with Greek soldiers. Many tried to run, and some escaped, but many were slain.

Deiphobus's house was far from the flames. I hurried there and found Helen, sitting beside her loom.

I was about to take off my Helmet when Menelaus strode into the room, his sword in his hand.

Helen looked up at him. "Menelaus," she said, "do you mean to slay me? No one would blame you."

Menelaus came closer to Helen. "No one would," he said.

Helen fell to her knees before her husband. "It was not my choice to leave you, Menelaus," she said. "But it was my fate. Aphrodite picked me to be with Paris, and Cupid cast a spell on me with his arrow so that I believed I loved him. When Paris died, at last the spell was broken."

"So Odysseus told me," said Menelaus, gazing down at Helen. He lowered his sword and took her hand. "Come. We must leave before all of Troy goes up in flames."

Together the two of them hurried through the smoke-filled streets and down to the ships. I hurried after them, glad to be out where the air was clear.

"I know it was your fate to leave me," Menelaus told Helen as they boarded his ship. "But it will take me some time to trust you again."

"We have a long voyage ahead of us," said Helen. "Perhaps by the time we reach Sparta we will understand each other again."

Menelaus smiled. "I hope so, Helen," he said. Then he went to give the crew orders to cast off.

Helen sat down near the bow of the ship. From under her robe she took a handloom and a skein of yarn as red as Menelaus's hair had once been and began to weave.

I watched Menelaus's ship sail off. When it was out of sight, I turned toward the burning ruins of Troy. At last the war was over, and it had ended as badly for the Trojans as Cassandra had said it would. It was time for me to go home.

ZZZZZZIP!

EPILOGUE

Now you know the real story of Helen of
Troy. And how my myth-o-maniac brother Zeus
twisted the truth to blame her for the Trojan War
when it wasn't her fault at all. Seriously, how can
that weasely god stand to live with himself?

I was happy that Helen and Menelaus finally
got back together again after the war. Helen
had been through a lot, as had Menelaus, so I
was hoping they'd have smooth sailing back to
Sparta and live happily every after.

But you know, mortal readers, myths aren't
fairy tales. There are very few happily ever afters
in the myths.

When the Greeks finally sailed away from Troy, the gods who'd had such a fun time taking sides and meddling in the war suddenly realized that all their temples inside Troy had been destroyed.

Of course they had! What did they think would happen in a war?

But Apollo, Athena, and the rest of them got all worked up about it. They couldn't very well be angry at the Trojans because, well, there weren't many Trojans left. So they took their anger out on the Greeks and sent wild winds to blow their ships off course.

Menelaus's ship was blown to Egypt, and he and Helen spent several years there, getting to know each other again.

After a while, the gods decided that the Greeks had been punished enough, and Po sent tailwinds to speed their ships home to Greece. When at last they reached Sparta, Menelaus and Helen took up their lives as king and queen much as they'd done before Paris came along.

Hermione had been only nine years old when

Helen took off with Paris, and the little girl had gone to live with her Aunt Clytemnestra. By the time Helen and Menelaus returned home, Hermione was a young woman of marriageable age.

Menelaus had promised Pyrrhus, the son of Achilles, that if he came to fight with the Greeks, he could have Hermione's hand in marriage. So it was no surprise when Pyrrhus showed up in Sparta to claim her for his bride. Pyrrhus had red hair, just like her father's, and Hermione liked that. What she never did learn to like was weaving.

When I finished writing *Hit the Road, Helen!* I was almost as exhausted as I'd been after spending a decade trying to stop the Trojan War.

One night when my queen and I were in the den, playing Scrabble, Persephone said, "You need a vacation, Hades."

She put tiles down on the board to spell the word *CRUISE*.

"A cruise?" I said. "I don't have time to go on a cruise."

"The Furies have gotten really good at taking care of things down here," Persephone went on. "You can take some time off, Hades. Wouldn't it be fun to spend the winter cruising around the warm, sunny Caribbean?"

She handed me a brochure that read:

IMMORTAL CRUISE LINES
WE'VE BEEN TAKING GOOD CARE OF GODS AND GODDESSES FOREVER!

"They serve ambrosia and nectar at every meal," Persephone added. "And you know what, Hades? We can do the whole thing on frequent flier miles."

It turned out that with all the astro-traveling I'd done, *ZZZZZZIPPING!* back and forth between the Underworld and Mount Olympus, and between Sparta and Troy, I'd racked up millions of points. How could I say no?

To my great surprise, I had the time of my godly life on that cruise! We sat in deck chairs all day, dozing and reading. And I was happy to discover that the Norse god Thor was on board, too. After spending so much time with Zeus and Hera and the crew from Mount Olympus, it was fun to meet some new deities who had new things to talk about.

Thor's a great guy, even if he is a thunder god like you-know-who. Instead of a bucket of lightning bolts, Thor makes thunder with this oversized hammer, which he insisted on carrying around everywhere on the ship.

Persephone was crazy about Thor's golden-haired wife, Sif, and the four of us had dinner together almost every night. I really wish you could see Thor in action at a buffet table, mortals. Whoa, that god can really put the food away! Immortal Cruise Lines totally took a bath on his ticket.

I spent some of my deck chair time thinking about which myth I wanted to debunk next. Inspired by being on that ship, I decided to tell the story of Jason and the Argonauts, who also went on a cruise of sorts.

The morning after we got home, I headed

straight to my Underworld office, a little cabin the ghost carpenters had built for me overlooking the Pool of Memory.

I was about halfway there when someone called my name. I turned and there was the ghost of Cassandra.

"Cassandra!" I said, surprised to see her. "What's wrong? Aren't you happy over in the apple orchards of Elysium?"

"Sure I am," said Cassandra. She began walking alongside me. "I love it there. Nothing ever happens, so I don't have to predict the future. It's perfect. But there's something I have to warn you about."

We'd reached my office. "Uh . . . you want to come inside?" I asked

Cassandra shook her head. "No, I'll make it quick," she said. "I know you're about to start your next book, but beware, Hades! Whatever you do, don't write about Jason and the Argonauts!"

"What?" I cried. "Why not?"

"If you write that book next," said Cassandra,

"nobody will buy it! And I mean *nobody*! Not even in the cheap e-book edition. It'll be a total flop."

"You're kidding!" I said.

Cassandra shook her head. "I don't do that sort of thing," she said.

"So I can never write about Jason and the Golden Fleece?" I asked.

"Did I say never?" said Cassandra. "I said *next*. It can't be next."

"I don't believe this," I said. Instantly I was sorry. Poor Cassandra's ghost looked as if she were going to burst into tears.

"Sorry, Cassandra," I said. "It's just that I took this great cruise, so I'm all charged up to write about a long sea voyage."

Now Cassandra's face lit up. "That's the other thing I wanted to tell you, Hades," she said. "The next book you write *will* be about a long sea voyage."

"But not Jason's voyage?" I asked.

"Don't even think it!" said Cassandra. "I'm talking about Odysseus's voyage."

"You mean the story of how he sailed away from Troy?" I asked. "And his ships were blown off course, and he had all sorts of crazy adventures?"

"That's the one," said Cassandra.

"Hmmm," I said. "It's an action-packed tale, that's for sure."

I started thinking about the time Odysseus was trapped in the cave of the Cyclopes. And the time he encountered the witch, Circe. It was a ripping good yarn, and I'd been there for lots of it, helping out my old pal.

"I believe you're right, Cassandra," I said.

"You believe me?" Cassandra cried ecstatically.

"Absolutely!" I said.

Her ghost grinned at me and then floated off in the direction of Elysium.

Inside my office, I pulled my copy of *The Big Fat Book of Greek Myths* off the shelf. I wanted to see what Zeus's rewrite nymphs had done to the story of Odysseus. I couldn't believe my godly eyes!

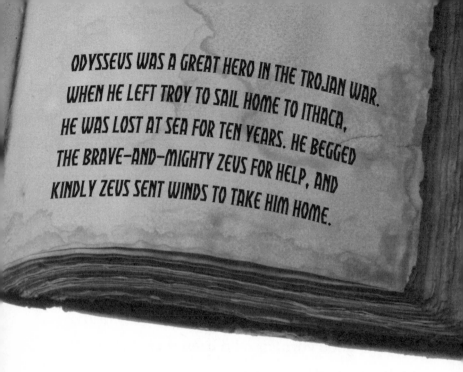

ODYSSEUS WAS A GREAT HERO IN THE TROJAN WAR. WHEN HE LEFT TROY TO SAIL HOME TO ITHACA, HE WAS LOST AT SEA FOR TEN YEARS. HE BEGGED THE BRAVE-AND-MIGHTY ZEUS FOR HELP, AND KINDLY ZEUS SENT WINDS TO TAKE HIM HOME.

Kindly Zeus? Whoever wrote that had clearly never met the Ruler of the Universe. And besides, Odysseus never asked Zeus for help. He asked Athena! The goddess of wisdom was a big champion of the clever Odysseus. And Zeus left out the reason for Odysseus's wanderings altogether — my bro Po. Take it from me; if you're a sailor, don't anger the god of the seas.

As I read, I knew I had to set the record straight. Sorry, Jason. You'll have to wait your turn. Right now, I have a story to write about Odysseus.

KING HADES'S
QUICK-AND-EASY
GUIDE TO THE MYTHS

Let's face it, mortals. When you read the Greek myths, you sometimes run into long, unpronounceable names like *Penthesilea* and *Hephaestus* — names so long and complicated that just looking at them can give you a great big headache. It can get pretty confusing. But never fear! I'm here to set you straight with my quick-and-easy guide to who's who and what's what in the myths.

Achilles (uh-KILL-eez) — son of Thetis and Peleus, the greatest Greek hero.

Agamemnon (ag-uh-MEM-non) — king of Mycenae and high king of Greece.

Amazons [AM-uh-zonz] — a nation of women warriors.

ambrosia (am-BRO-zha) — food that we gods must eat to stay young and good-looking for eternity.

Aphrodite (af-ruh-DIE-tee) — goddess of love and beauty; supported Troy in the war.

Apollo (uh-POL-oh) — god of light, music, and poetry; tried to help the Trojans win.

Asphodel Fields (AS-fo-del FEELDZ) — large weedy region of the Underworld; home to the ghosts of those who were not so good, but not so bad on earth.

Athena (uh-THE-nuh) — goddess of wisdom, weaving, and war; supported the Greeks.

Aulis (AW-liss) — the ancient harbor the Greek army set sail from during the Trojan War.

Calchas (KAL-kuhs) — a Trojan prophet who joins the Greeks during the Trojan War.

Cassandra (kuh-SAN-druh) — King Priam's daughter and Paris's sister; foretells the future, but no one believes her.

Cerberus (SIR-buh-rus) — my fine, III-headed pooch; guard dog of the Underworld.

Charon (CARE-un) — River Taxi driver; ferries the living and the dead across the River Styx.

Clytemnestra (kly-tem-NES-tra) — Helen's sister; wife of Agamemnon.

Deiphobus (die-FO-bus) — brother of Paris.

drosis (DRO-sis) — short for *theoexidrosis* (thee-oh-ex-ih-DRO-sis); old Greek speak for "violent god sweat."

Elysium (eye-LIHZ-ee-um) — Underworld region for ghosts of the good.

Eris (AIR-uhs) — goddess of discord who threw the golden apple.

Furies (FYOOR-eez) — winged, red-eyed, snake-haired immortals who pursue and punish wrongdoers; around my palace, they're known as Tisi, Meg, and Alec.

Hades (HEY-deez) — Ruler of the Underworld, Lord of the Dead, King Hades, that's me. I'm also god of wealth and an author.

Hector (HEK-tur) — son of Priam, brother of Paris, greatest Trojan hero.

Helen (HEL-uhn) — the beautiful mortal daughter of Zeus; wife of Menelaus who ran off with Paris.

Hephaestus (huh-FESS-tus) — god of fire and the forge; married to Aphrodite.

Hera (HERE-uh) — Zeus's wife, Queen of the gods, supporter of the Greeks.

Hercules (HER-kew-leez) — Roman name for the son of Zeus who became immortal.

Hermes (HER-meez) — messenger of the gods, especially Zeus.

Hermione (her-MY-oh-nee) — daughter of Helen and Menelaus.

Hypnos (HIP-nos) — god of sleep.

ichor (EYE-ker) — god blood.

immortal (i-MOR-tuhl) — a being, such as a god or a monster, who will never die, like me.

Laocoon (la-oh-COO-on) — Trojan priest killed by serpents for attacking the wooden horse.

Leda (LEE-duh) — white-armed queen of Sparta; mother of Helen.

Menelaus (men-uh-LAY-uhs) — husband of Helen; Agamemnon's brother; King of Sparta.

mortal (MOR-tuhl) — a being that will die. I hate to break it to you, but you are a mortal.

Mount Olympus (oh-LIM-pess) — highest mountain in Greece; its peak is home to all major gods, except for my brother Po and me.

Myrmidons (MUR-mi-donz) — a group of incredibly brave, skilled warriors in Greece who were led by Achilles in the Trojan War.

nectar (NECK-ter) — what we gods drink to make us look good and feel godly.

Nereid (NEE-re-id) — sea nymphs; daughters of Nereus.

Nereus (NEE-ree-us) — Old Man of the Sea; father of Thetis.

Nestor (NES-tur) — the oldest and wisest of all the Greek heroes.

Odysseus (oh-DISS-ee-uhs) — King of Ithaca and the cleverest Greek hero.

Palamedes (pal-uh-MED-es) — a crafty Greek

hero who rounded up Odysseus for the Trojan
War.

Palladium (puh-LEY-dee-uhm) — a statue of
Athena that resided in Troy; the safety of the
city supposedly depended upon it.

Paris (PAIR-uhs) — son of Priam, snappy
dresser, brought Helen to Troy.

Patroclus (puh-TROH-kluhs) — Achilles's
closest friend; killed in battle by Hector.

Peleus (PEA-lee-us) — husband of Thetis,
father of Achilles; commander of Myrmidon.

Penelope (puh-NELL-uh-pea) — Helen's
cousin, Odysseus's wife.

Penthesilea (pen-thes-i-LEE-a) — Queen of
the Amazons.

Persephone (per-SEF-uh-nee) — goddess of
spring and Queen of the Underworld.

Philoctetes (fil-uhk-TEE-teez) — great
friend of Hercules, who inherited his Bow
and Arrows; abandoned on an island by the
Greeks.

Poseidon (po-SIGH-den) — my bro Po; god of the seas and friend of the Greeks.

Priam (PRAHY-uhm) — King of Troy; father of Hector and Paris as well as 48 more sons and daughters.

Pyrrhus (PIE-rus) — son of Achilles.

Roman numerals (ROH-muhn NOO-mur-uhlz) — what the ancients used instead of counting on their fingers. Makes you glad you live in the age of Arabic numerals and calculators, doesn't it?

I	1	XI	11	XXX	30
II	2	XII	12	XL	40
III	3	XIII	13	L	50
IV	4	XIV	14	LX	60
V	5	XV	15	LXX	70
VI	6	XVI	16	LXXX	80
VII	7	XVII	17	XC	90
VIII	8	XVIII	18	C	100
IX	9	XIX	19	D	500
X	10	XX	20	M	1000

Sarpedon (sahr-PEE-don) — mortal son of Zeus; killed in battle by Patroclus.

Sinon (SAHY-non) — Greek soldier who tricked the Trojans into bringing the Trojan Horse into their city.

Tartarus (TAR-tar-us) — the deepest pit in the Underworld and home of the Punishment Fields, where burning flames and red-hot lava eternally torment the ghosts of the wicked.

Thetis (THEE-tis) — powerful Nereid; married to Peleus; mother of Achilles.

Tisi (TIZ-ee) — see **Furies**.

Tyndareus (TYN-dar-us) — husband of Leda; earthly father of Helen.

Underworld (UHN-dur-wurld) — my very own kingdom, where the ghosts of dead mortals come to spend eternity.

Zeus (ZOOSE) — rhymes with goose, which pretty much says it all; my little brother, a major myth-o-maniac and a cheater, who managed to set himself up as Ruler of the Universe.

THE BIG FAT BOOK OF GREEK MYTHS

According to ancient Greek mythology, Helen, the mortal daughter of Zeus and Leda, was the most beautiful woman in the world. When it was time for her to marry, kings and princes from around the world came to court her, including Odysseus, King of Ithaca.

Before a winner was chosen, Odysseus made the rest of her suitors swear an oath to defend the honor of Helen's future husband, no matter what. Helen eventually married a Greek king, Menelaus of Sparta, and they lived happily together for many years.

But everything changed when Paris, a prince of Troy, came to visit Sparta. Aphrodite had promised Paris that the most beautiful woman in the world would fall in love with him as a reward for naming her the fairest of all the goddesses. And so it was that Helen fell in love with Paris and ran off to Troy with him while her husband was away.

When Menelaus discovered his wife was missing, he was determined to get her back. He called on Helen's original suitors to fulfill their oaths and fight with him to bring Helen back to Sparta.

The Greeks assembled their armies and sailed to Troy, where they fought for ten long years to take the city. But no matter what they did, the Trojans remained safe behind the high wall that surrounded the city.

Finally Odysseus, the cleverest of all Greek heroes, came up with an idea to get inside the city: the Trojan Horse. Greek soldiers hid inside the belly of an enormous wooden horse and tricked the Trojans into thinking they'd sailed home. When the Trojans brought the horse inside the city, the Greeks attacked.

One of the Trojans, Aeneas, a nephew of King Priam, is said to have escaped the city. He led the surviving Trojans to modern-day Italy, where he became the founder of Rome.

KATE MCMULLAN is the author of the chapter book series Dragon Slayers' Academy, as well as easy readers featuring Fluffy, the Classroom Guinea Pig. She and her illustrator husband, Jim McMullan, have created several award-winning picture books, including *I STINK!*, *I'M DIRTY!*, and *I'M BIG!* Her latest work is *SCHOOL! Adventures at Harvey N. Trouble Elementary* in collaboration with the famed *New Yorker* cartoonist George Booth. Kate and Jim live in Sag Harbor, NY, with two bulldogs and a mews named George.

GLOSSARY

comrades (KOM-radz) — good friends or colleagues

cunning (KUHN-ing) — clever at tricking other people

discord (DISS-kord) — disagreement between two or more people

eternal (i-TUR-nuhl) — lasting forever

invincible (in-VIN-suh-buhl) — unable to be beaten or defeated

morph (MORF) — to change shape into something else

occasion (uh-KAY-zhuhn) — a special or important event

occupation (ok-yuh-PAY-shuhn) — a job

prophecy (PROF-uh-see) — a prediction

seer (SEE-ur) — a person who predicts future events

suitor (SOO-tur) — a man who courts a woman

DISCUSS!

I. There were many great heroes on both sides of the Trojan War. Talk about who your favorite was and why.

II. Zeus tried to lay all the blame for the Trojan War on Helen in his version of the story. Do you think Helen was at fault? Talk about your opinion.

III. My meddling siblings just couldn't resist choosing sides in the Trojan War. Do you think it was right of the gods to help the Greeks and Trojans? Why or why not?

WRITE!

I. Paris had to make a difficult choice between three very opinionated goddesses. Write about what you would have done if Zeus asked you to award the apple to the fairest goddess. Who would you have picked?

II. Odysseus comes up with the idea to trick the Trojans using the Trojan Horse. Write about a clever trick you pulled on someone.

III. Imagine that you are Helen. Write about leaving Sparta and arriving in Troy from her point of view.

MYTH-O-MANIA

I

II

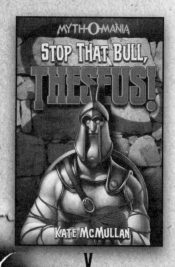

V

VI

READ THE REST OF THE SERIES AND LEARN THE REAL STORIES!

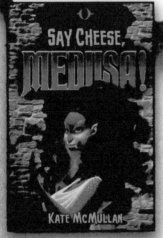

III

IV

VII

VII

THE FUN DOESN'T STOP HERE!

DISCOVER MORE:

Videos & Contests!
Games & Puzzles!
Heroes & Villains!
Authors & Illustrators!

@ www.CAPSTONEKIDS.com